Andy Griffiths discovered a talent for being stupid at an early age. Since then he has amazed the world with a truly stunning array of minor mistakes, major miscalculations, idiotic acts, inane remarks, incomprehensible behaviour and extremely stupid stories. He has written two other titles in the Just! series—*Just Tricking!* and *Just Annoying!*

Terry Denton was born in Venezuela in 1909. He sailed on the maiden voyage of the *Titanic* in 1912 and was lost at sea. He came back to life in 1932, working as an ironing board for Mrs Ida Bugg of Wisconsin, USA. He would have been the first ironing board to conquer Mt Everest, but for a nasty bus accident on the way to the airport. Reincarnated (again) in 1963, he worked as a hostess on *Snail of the Century*, before retiring to illustrate children's books. In 1985, he gave birth to quintuplets. He now lives a quiet life with his six quintuplets between the covers of this stupid book.

Stupid dumb near-naked author.

Brilliant, clever, talented illustrator.

Guide to inside-front Photo.

Visit Andy's Website:
www.andygriffiths.com.au

JUST STUPID!

ANDY GRIFFITHS

with illustrations by Terry Denton

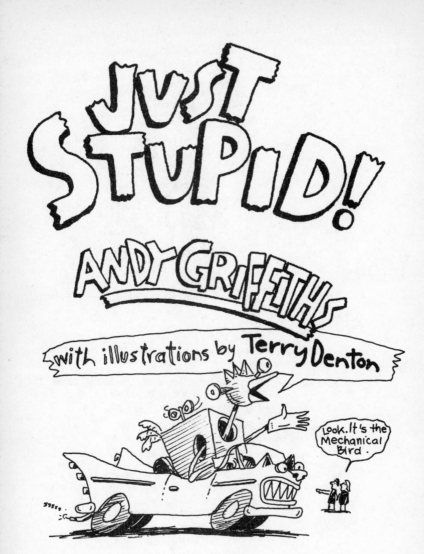

Look. It's the Mechanical Bird.

PAN

Pan Macmillan Australia

First published 1999 in Pan by Pan Macmillan Australia Pty Limited
St Martins Tower, 31 Market St, Sydney

Reprinted 1999 (twice), 2000 (three times)

Text Copyright © Andy Griffiths 1999
Illustrations Copyright © Terry Denton 1999

National Library of Australia
cataloguing-in-publication data:

Griffiths, Andy, 1961– .
Just stupid.

ISBN 0 330 36148 1.

I. Denton, Terry, 1950– . II. Title.

A823.3

Typeset in 12/16pt New Aster by Post Pre-press Group
Printed in Australia by McPherson's Printing Group

Contents

We do hope you have enjoyed the CONTENTS PAGE. feel free to return at any time for another read.

BUSTING

I'm in the supermarket trying to remember what groceries Mum wanted me to pick up, but I can't think. I can't breathe. I can't do anything. I'm busting. And I don't mean busting. I mean BUSTING!

I've got to find a toilet. Fast. Then I can come back and think about the shopping with a clear head. Or not so much a clear head as an empty bladder.

I haven't got a second to lose. I run down the aisle and skid round the corner.

WHAM!

Straight into an old guy with a walking frame. He staggers forward and crashes into a stack of cans. They go rolling all over the floor. The old man is lying in the middle of them.

Hi! I'm the PAGE NUMBER SNAIL.

RUNAWAY PRAM. INTERACTIVE MOVIE. Grasp book between thumb + forefinger and FLICK!

'Well, don't just stand there,' he says. 'Help me up!'

I reach down, take hold of his hand and pull him to his feet. Luckily he's not very heavy. I stand his walking frame up for him. He's muttering words I don't understand.

The store manager appears. I can tell he's the store manager because his pants are too tight. Plus he's wearing a badge that says Store Manager.

'What happened?' he says.

Before I can say anything the old man answers.

'This silly young boy knocked me over. It wouldn't have happened in my day. When I was young we respected our elders.'

'It was an accident!' I say.

'Were you running?' says the store manager.

'Yes,' I say, 'but I'm . . .'

'There's no excuse,' he says. 'I think you owe this gentleman an apology. Then you can pick up all the cans.'

'But I'm busting!'

'You should have thought about that before you started knocking people over and destroying my displays,' he says.

I get the feeling that I'm going to get out

of here quicker if I just do what he says. I turn to the old man.

'I'm sorry,' I say. 'I shouldn't have been running and I hope you're not hurt.'

WHAT IS THE NEXT WORD in this series?

+ POW!
+ SLAM!
+ FZzzP!
+ ----
Ans: Pg 93

He shrugs and mutters something else that I can't understand. I start picking up the cans. I can't believe how far they've rolled. Some have rolled at least two or three aisles away. And the store manager makes me pick up every last one.

By the time I've finished I'm seriously busting.

But I know better than to run out of the store. This time I just walk very quickly.

I get outside the supermarket and into the main shopping centre. I'm looking for a sign pointing to the toilets. I can't see one.

There is a man selling pencils outside the supermarket.

'Excuse me,' he says. 'Want to buy a pencil?'

'No thanks,' I say.

'They're cheap—twenty cents each.'

'No thank you,' I say.

'Just one,' he says. 'One lousy pencil!'

'I haven't got time!' I say.

'You could have bought one by now,' he says.

2 This is really Page 3. But I'm a slow snail.

For information on HOW TO WIN A LIFETIME'S SUPPLY OF FREEZER BAGS, turn to Page 186.

What kind of freezer bags?

MOO

'How many times do I have to say it?' I say. 'I don't want—or need—a pencil. What I need is a toilet. I'm busting!'

His shoulders drop. He sighs heavily. He looks like he's going to cry. If he's trying to make me feel bad then he's succeeding.

'Okay,' I say, fumbling for change. 'I'll have a pencil.'

I can't find a twenty-cent piece. All I can find is a two dollar coin.

'Have you got change?' I say.

'No,' he says. 'You're the first one to buy a pencil today.'

'Keep the change then,' I say.

'No, that wouldn't be right,' he says. 'I'm not looking for charity.'

'Fine,' I say, 'give me ten pencils!'

He counts the pencils out really slowly, one by one. He makes a mistake and has to start again. I'm shifting from foot to foot.

Finally he hands the pencils to me.

'Have a great day,' he says.

'I will if I don't bust,' I say. I run off before he figures out another way to waste my time.

I'm running as fast as I can, but I'm not sure where to. I have no idea where the toilets are. This shopping centre is too big.

2
Phew! Page 4. I can't keep up.

There are too many levels. Too many people getting in my way. I want to scream.

I trip and stumble. I look down. My shoelaces have come undone. I hate my shoelaces. It doesn't matter how well I tie them up, they just keep coming undone. I can't ignore them, either, because they're extra long laces. Now I have to stop and waste valuable toilet-searching seconds doing them up.

SHOPPING HINTS.

- Go into the butcher's shop.
- Ask them if they sell meat.
- Ask them how much it is.
- Do they have any Fresian?
- Does it come with chips?
- Can you have it in a cone?

I kneel down. It's not easy. It's putting pressure on a part of my body that's already under too much strain. I grab the laces and pull them tight. I loop them around each other. Then I loop the loops together and pull them tight as well. That should hold it. At least for a little while. I do the other shoe. I try to stand up. It hurts even more than kneeling down. I don't have much time.

Suddenly, hanging overhead, I find the sign I've been looking for. A picture of a man, a woman, a wheelchair and an arrow pointing to the left. I turn and sprint down a little corridor. I can see the toilets up ahead of me.

Oh no. I don't believe it. There's a yellow plastic pyramid outside the toilet.

Closed for cleaning!

2

Page 5!! Please don't tell the author, he'll fire me.

It's never a good time to clean a toilet.

Of all the times to clean a toilet, why now? Why not at night when there's nobody here?

Should I try to find another toilet or just wait?

I'll wait.

But I'm busting.

I can't wait.

But I can't not wait.

I have to go. Right now.

Why does life have to be so difficult?

Hang on! The handicapped toilet is not closed.

Can you go to jail for using a handicapped person's toilet when you're not really handicapped? Surely not. I'm sure nobody would mind. I'm busting so bad I'm practically handicapped anyway.

I hobble up to the door and push it open. It's vacant. I want to go in but something is stopping me. It would be so easy to just slip in here, and yet, so wrong.

If I get away with using this toilet, who's to say where or when it will stop? I could be taking the first step towards a life of crime. Today the handicapped toilets—tomorrow I'll be leaving my bike in the spaces reserved for handicapped drivers and walking up disabled

2
Page 6, and what's this? A skateboard.

access ramps instead of taking the stairs.

I can't do it. I let go of the door. I might be busting, but I'm not a criminal.

'Hey!' yells a voice. 'You can't use that toilet! You're not handicapped!'

BAA CODE

I turn around. Oh no. It's the old guy with the walking frame. He's hobbling up the corridor towards me.

'I'm not going to use it,' I say, backing away from the door.

'Then why did you have the door open?' he says.

'Well, I *was* going to use it but . . .'

'A-ha! I thought so,' he says. 'Tearing around the supermarket and knocking people over. Using the handicapped people's toilets and stopping the truly handicapped from using them. You're a menace to society. I'm going to call a security guard!'

I nearly blubbered when I saw this whale-meat joke.

'No!' I say. 'I'm not a menace—I'm just busting!'

But the old man is not listening.

'Help! Guards! Arrest this boy!'

He's crazy. I've got to get out of here. He's creating such a racket you'd think he was being murdered or something.

I run down the corridor and back into the

5

PAGE 7... catching up!!

shopping centre. I'm not sure where I'm going. I need to find a location map.

I pass a shop with an enormous poster of a river in the front window. It's an ad for a video called *Great Rivers of the World*. If I don't find a toilet fast there'll be one more great river in the world. Right here in the shopping centre.

I can't hold out much longer. I can hear splashing. Uh-oh. I look down.

No, it's not coming from me. That's a relief. Well, sort of.

I look around. It's coming from the indoor fountain. There are about fifty thousand jets of water spraying in every direction. The sound of all that water is excruciating, but it does give me an idea. Maybe I could go in the fountain. I could get in, stand in the middle and pretend to be a statue. I could squirt water out of my mouth at the same time. Nobody will even realise.

But hang on! In front of the fountain is a map of the shopping centre. Fantastic!

I hobble over to the map. Hmmm. There are about half a million shops spread across three levels. So there are actually three maps. Lower, middle and upper with letters and numbers around the border of each one. It's very complicated.

And the sound of all that splashing is not making it any easier to concentrate. Whose idea was it to put a fountain inside a shopping centre anyway? I'd like to find that person and tell them they made a big mistake. And I'd like to find the person who made the shopping centre. I think they made the biggest mistake of all.

This shopping centre is way too big. I mean do we really need button shops? Or shops that sell nothing except stuff made out of cane? And as if there aren't already more than enough shops to buy gifts in, some genius comes up with the idea of a gift shop. As far as I'm concerned, the only thing more stupid than a gift shop is a shop that sells nothing but cat ornaments—and there's one of those here as well.

It doesn't help that the front of the map is suddenly smeared with water. I turn around. Two little kids are squirting each other with water pistols.

'Quit it!' I say.

They don't reply. They just squirt me. Right in the front of my pants.

9

There's a guy wearing a rainbow-coloured shirt standing next to me. He looks like a hippie but I'll ask him anyway. That's how desperate I am.

'Excuse me,' I say.

He turns towards me. His eyes are half-closed. He looks like he hasn't slept for about three weeks.

'Can you help me find the toilets?' I say.

'Looks like it's a bit late,' he says in a slow voice.

'What do you mean?' I say.

He points to the front of my pants.

'That's not what you think it is,' I say. 'But it will be if you don't help me find the toilets.'

'Chill out, man,' says the hippie. He turns back to the map and studies it carefully. 'Says here the toilets are at M 16 on level two.'

'What level are we on now?' I say.

'Ummm, level three,' he says, squinting at the map. 'No, hang on ... level one ... oops—make that level four.'

'Level four?' I say. 'There's no such level!'

'Hey, man,' says the hippie, 'open your mind. There are many levels. More levels than you ever dreamed of.'

'Are you insane?' I say.

KNOCK

10

OH! OH!

'Relax,' he says. 'Take it easy.'

'I can't!' I yell. 'I'm busting! I've got to get to a toilet! Quick!'

AMAZING TOILET TRICKS: #27.
Forward 2½ twist dive.

'No man, you're missing the point,' he says. 'The destination's not important. The journey is where it's at.'

'Not when you're busting it's not,' I say.

I can't stand still any longer. I start running. I see an escalator going up. I jump on.

I don't believe it. It's almost too good to be true. At the top of the escalator is a sign. A man, a woman and a wheelchair.

I bound up the last few steps and leap off the escalator. Suddenly my leg is jerked backwards.

I look behind me.

My shoelace is caught in the top of the escalator! I try to pull my foot away, but I can't. The lace is in too deep.

I have to unlace my shoe.

I bend down and poke my finger in between the tongue and the lace. But I can't pull the lace out because the escalator has grabbed the other end of it as well. My finger is trapped.

The laces are being pulled tighter and tighter. My finger is going bright red. It's throbbing.

11

Another fine mess...

Great! Now I'm busting *and* I've got my shoelace stuck in an escalator *and* my finger stuck in my shoe.

I have to get my shoe off. I don't care about my shoe. All I care about is . . . well you know what I care about.

I put the index finger of my other hand into the back of my shoe to try to lever my heel out.

Oh no.

I don't believe it.

I can't get my finger out of the back of the shoe. The shoe is getting tighter. And tighter. And tighter.

The escalator is sucking. And sucking. And sucking.

There's nothing I can do, apart from chew my foot off. That's it! Chewing! Only I don't have to chew through my ankle . . . just my shoelace.

I bend right down. I'm trying to get close enough to the lace to take a good bite. All of a sudden my scalp starts burning. My hair is caught in the escalator!

This is like the most impossible and painful game of Twister ever. I'm bent over double, looking upside down through my legs.

Oh no.

The old man is coming up the escalator. He's got his walking frame held out in front of him. He's coming right for me.

He hits me fair and square in the bum.

I tumble forward. The shoelace has snapped and a huge chunk of my hair has been ripped out, but I don't care. I'm free!

'Now we're even!' shouts the old man.

'No we're not,' I say, scrambling to my feet, 'because you just did me a big favour!'

He looks dumbfounded.

I start running.

I'm almost there. Only a few metres more. Something is stabbing me in the leg. What is that? I put my hand into my pocket.

Aaaggh! Something jabs me in the thumb. It's those stupid pencils. They're too sharp. Like little spears. They could do me a serious injury in there. As I pull them out of my pocket they spill onto the ground in front of me. Uh-oh. Bad move. I'm going too fast to stop. I slip up on them and fall backwards. I whack my head.

Next thing I know I'm being shaken awake. I open my eyes. A fireman is kneeling beside me. The corridor is filled with smoke and I can hear sirens.

'Wake up!' says the fireman. 'Are you okay?'

'What?' I say. 'What's happening?'

He lifts me to my feet. I slip on a pencil and fall back down.

'You have to get out of here,' he says. 'Fire!'

He lifts me up again and starts shepherding me towards the exit. Away from the toilet!

I try to head back towards the toilet but he grabs me.

'Wrong way,' he says, pointing towards the exit. 'That way.'

'But I have to go to the toilet,' I say, 'I'm busting!'

'You'll have to wait,' says the fireman. 'It's not safe! You have to get out of the building.'

'Not safe?!' I say. 'If I don't get to the toilet soon, nobody will be safe. This shopping centre will be flooded!'

But he's not listening. He's escorting me to the exit.

Outside there are four fire trucks in a row. The firemen are spraying enormous arcs of water onto the building. It might be helping to extinguish the fire but it's definitely not helping me.

IN CASE OF FIRE:

TAKE PROPER PRECAUTIONS

AVOID PANIC

ASSIST OTHERS

PADDLE CALMLY TO THE EXITS

14

I overhear the fire chief talking on his walkie-talkie.

'All we know is that the fire appears to have started in one of the escalators,' he says. 'Some foreign material may have got in there and shorted the system. Until we can put the fire out we can't be sure. But to do that we're going to need back-up units . . . as many as you've got.'

As a CHIEF FIRE OFFICER I object to this STUPID and unrealistic attempt at FIRE CONTROL. The author's just being stupid!!

He wipes the sweat off his brow.

Suddenly I know what I have to do. I can solve my problem and be a hero at the same time.

'Excuse me,' I say, 'you're not going to need those back-up units.'

'What are you talking about?' he says.

'You've got me,' I say.

'Huh?'

I'm JUST STUPIDER

'Watch this!' I say.

I go as close to the burning building as I can. I grab hold of my fly. I take aim.

Ahhhhhhhhhhhhhhhh. Relief! Beautiful relief! The fire is powerless against me. It disappears in clouds of steam. People are gathered around applauding. The supermarket manager is there. And the pencil seller. And the hippie. Even the old man. Cheering.

15

MMPH

He He

Chanting my name. I don't know how they know my name but I don't care about that right now. All I care about is how good this feels. And how warm. It's so warm.

I roll over and snuggle down deeper into my blankets. My blankets? What are my blankets doing here? And why am I wearing pyjamas?

I blink a few times. I rub my eyes.

There's no shopping centre. There are no fire trucks. No people.

I'm in my bedroom. In my bed. Wrapped in my blankets. Putting out a fire. Only there's no fire either.

I hate that.

16

I mean it.

expel me!

DANGER:
Beware the
smiling
Principal.

it's the first day back at school.

And if all goes to plan it will also be my last.

I'm sitting up the back corner of the classroom. Well, I'm not really sitting. I'm leaning back on the chair, putting all my weight on the back legs, just like we're not supposed to.

And that's not the only rule I'm breaking.

My feet are up on the desk. I'm not wearing any shoes. I'm wearing a cap. My T-shirt is ripped. Plus it has a rude slogan on the front. I've got my Walkman on. On the table in front of me is a packet of bubblegum, a spitball shooter and some freshly chewed spitballs. On the blackboard I've drawn this crazy-looking stick figure with bugged-out

GRRRRR

SNAIL-FREE ZONE.

eyes and buck teeth. It's hitting itself over the head with a hammer and saying 'Look at me—I'm your stupid new teacher!' And underneath it I've written 'By Andy Griffiths' so that there's no chance anybody else will get the blame.

I figure the new teacher will be like all new teachers. They'll be wanting to show everybody how tough they are. They won't be wanting to muck around with warnings or detentions or phone calls to parents. They'll be looking for a scapegoat to send straight to the principal's office. Well, they won't have to look for long. Here I am—ready and willing.

Danny comes into the room. He looks at me and his mouth falls open.

'Are you crazy?' he finally says. He's obviously having trouble taking in the full extent of my badness.

'No,' I say.

'But your feet . . . your T-shirt . . . the spit-ball shooter . . .' splutters Danny. 'Boy, are you going to cop it!'

'Good,' I say. 'I want to cop it. I want to be expelled.'

'Expelled?' he says.

'I'm sick of school,' I say.

'But it's only the first day back,' he says. 'And school hasn't even started yet. How can you be sick of it?'

'Are you kidding?' I say. 'I can't live like this. Bells, timetables, lessons, rules and regulations—they're not for me. I had a taste of freedom on the holidays and I decided I'm not coming back.'

'But you're here,' says Danny.

'Only long enough to get myself expelled,' I say. 'Then I'm out of school for good.'

'But your parents will just send you somewhere else,' says Danny.

'You don't get it, Dan, do you?' I say. 'If my parents try that I'll just get myself expelled from there as well.'

Danny smiles.

'You reckon it's that easy?' he says.

'Of course it is,' I say. 'What could be easier? It's not like there's any shortage of rules to break.'

'You're not wrong there,' says Danny, nodding.

'And when you think about it,' I say, 'how hard is it to break a rule?'

'It's not hard,' says Danny, now shaking his head. 'It's not hard at all.'

19 Up there.

'Better to die on your feet than live on your knees,' I say.

'Yeah,' says Danny, 'you're right. Because living on your knees would be really uncomfortable. Your pants would wear out and your knees would get all scabby, and it would take ages to get anywhere . . .'

'We *are* living on our knees, Dan,' I say. 'But not me. Not any longer. I'm walking out of here.'

Danny looks at me, his eyes shining.

'Can I get expelled with you?' he says.

'Sure,' I say. 'Between us we can break twice as many rules as I could on my own. We'll be out of here in no time.'

'All right!' says Danny.

'It's a deal!' I say, holding out my hand. 'Give me the secret shake.'

'What is it again?' says Danny, bending over and putting his hand through his leg. 'Is this right?'

'No, Dan,' I say, 'that's the old one. Honestly, what's the point of having a secret handshake if you can never remember it?'

'Well it's been a while,' he says, 'what with the holidays and everything.'

I'm about to show him when a woman

20

An interesting waffly shape.

comes into the room. She must be our new teacher.

'Quick—get into position,' I say. 'Don't worry about the handshake. And don't forget to take your shoes off.'

I lean back on my chair. The new teacher is holding an old-fashioned projector and a small yellow slide box.

'Good morning,' she says. 'My name is Ms Livingstone. Sorry I'm a little late. I had a bit of trouble finding the room. I flew in very late last night and I didn't get much sleep. I was supposed to arrive a few weeks ago, but the yacht I was sailing was destroyed by a tsunami in the middle of the Pacific Ocean. I was marooned on a tiny island for many days before the rescue helicopters saw my smoke signals. I was beginning to give up hope that they would find me before the school term started. But, as you can see, here I am, safe and sound—just a little tired.'

Excited murmuring breaks out all around the room.

I think they actually believe her!

I look at Danny and roll my eyes.

'As if!' I say.

She probably just slept in. Just like I'll be

doing tomorrow morning. In a minute she'll see the blackboard . . . then she'll ask who Andy is . . . then she'll see me and Danny and before we know it we'll be on a one-way trip to the principal's office. This is too easy.

She still hasn't noticed me—too busy fussing around with the stuff on her desk. She hasn't seen the blackboard. I have to get her to turn around.

'Would you like me to clean the blackboard for you?' I say.

'Yes, thank you,' she says without looking at it—or me.

'Okay,' I say, stomping up the aisle as loudly as I can and swinging my arms in the stupidest and most attention-getting walk I can manage.

As I'm walking, I accidentally knock Lisa Mackney's folder off her table. It goes flying, hits the floor and the pages spill out everywhere. Lisa stares at me. I wish this had happened to anybody's folder but Lisa's.

'I'm sorry, Lisa,' I whisper.

I get down on my knees and start gathering up the paper. I push it all into the folder as neatly as I can.

'That's really nice of you to help pick all

Page 22

'that up,' says Ms Livingstone. 'You must be quite a gentleman.'

'But it was me who knocked it off in the first place,' I say.

'We all make mistakes,' she says.

'But I did it on purpose,' I say.

She laughs.

'I can't believe that somebody as helpful as you would do a thing like that,' she says. 'And even if you did, I'm sure you had a very good reason for it.'

'No I didn't,' I say. 'I did it because I'm bad and evil and I deserve to be sent straight to the principal's office.'

Ms Livingstone laughs again. She thinks I'm joking.

'Look at the board if you don't believe me,' I say.

Ms Livingstone looks at the board.

'That's very amusing,' she says. 'Who is it supposed to be?'

'It's you!' I say.

'Me?' she says. 'It doesn't look anything like me.'

She picks up a piece of chalk and, with just a few quick lines and squiggles, draws a perfect caricature of herself.

TO BE REALLY MEAN, YOU MUST:

Headbutt lamp posts.

Chew the heads off puppies.

PUSH OVER INTERNATIONAL ICONS.

Refuse to eat your Broccoli.

ANDY G by TERRY D

'That's me,' she says.

The whole class is laughing. Even me.

Then she draws another figure with a really crazy face. Boy, is it ugly and stupid-looking. It's much better than the one I drew.

'And that's you,' she says.

The class laughs even harder. I stop laughing.

'So you're not angry?' I say.

HEADGEAR

'Angry?' she says. 'Of course not. I'm flattered that you've gone to so much trouble to welcome me.'

'Well,' I say, 'aren't you at least going to tell me off for wearing my cap inside?'

'No,' she says, 'I find the fluorescent light very harsh myself. I don't blame you.'

I'm thrusting out my chest.

'What about my T-shirt?' I ask.

For a REALLY OFFENSIVE T-SHIRT SLOGAN TURN TO PAGE 105.

'What about it?' she says.

'It's got an offensive slogan on it,' I say.

Ms Livingstone laughs.

'Who would be offended by that?' she says.

'Anybody who reads it, I guess,' I say.

'Well, not necessarily,' she says. 'Whether something is offensive is very much in the eye of the beholder. For example, in our culture burping is considered offensive—but in some cultures not to burp after a meal is a dire insult to the host. Once, when I was travelling in Saudi Arabia I was invited to dine with Sheik Achmed Ben Bala. It was a magnificent feast but afterwards I was almost put to death because I was unable to show my appreciation by burping.'

The class gasps.

'It wasn't until he had the scimitar at my throat,' she continues, 'that I was able to reach deep within myself and produce the burp that saved my life. After three months in Saudi Arabia I became quite an expert.'

She gulps some air and lets forth with the most earsplitting burp I've ever heard. It's even louder than one of Danny's.

The whole class applauds. But not me. I can fake-burp any time I feel like it. It's no big deal.

I stomp back to my desk.

There must be some way to annoy her. I know—I'll ask some stupid questions.

'Excuse me, Ms Livingstone,' I say without putting my hand up.

'Yes?'

'Have you ever been to Germany?'

'Yes,' she says, 'I have.'

'Do people get sick a lot in Germany?'

'No more than other places, I expect,' she says. 'Why do you ask?'

'I just thought with all the *germs* and everything . . .'

The class erupts with laughter.

One to me.

Ms Livingstone runs her hand through her hair.

'Well, that's actually a very interesting question you've raised, Andy,' she says. 'Standards of health vary all over the world. For instance, when I was living with the Eskimos, I noticed that . . .'

Danny leans forward.

'You lived with Eskimos?' he says. 'In an igloo?'

'Oh yes,' she says. 'I was part of an expedition searching for the Abominable Snowman.'

The whole class is silent while she explains. One to her.

'Dan,' I say. 'Dan!'

But he can't hear me. He's too involved in Ms Livingstone's story. To tell you the truth, it is quite interesting. Especially the stuff about falling into the crevasse and trying to light a fire with only one match and a handful of wet wood—but that's not the point. We want to be expelled! Or at least I do. Danny can stay here if he wants. I've got things to do, places to be. I'm not sure what they are yet but I'll think of something.

I might as well stop beating around the bush.

'Ms Livingstone?' I say.

'Yes, Andy?'

'Can I be expelled?'

'I'm sorry, Andy, but I don't have the power to do that. That's a matter for the principal.'

'Can you send me to him?' I say.

'But why?' she says. 'What have you done wrong? What rules have you broken?'

'What rules *haven't* I broken!' I say, getting out my school diary. I start reading: ' "No leaning back on chairs. No feet on tables. No hats inside. No offensive slogans on clothing. No eating in class. Show respect to teachers. Show respect to fellow students and their property. No Walkmans. No banging. No tapping. No spitballs." I've broken every rule there is and it's not even recess!'

Ms Livingstone stands there thinking. She's got to send me to the principal's office now. She has no choice.

27

'Rules are very interesting things,' she says. 'It is important to have rules and laws and to obey them . . . but it is also important to know when to break them. In fact, sometimes, your life can depend on not obeying a rule or a law.'

Uh-oh, here we go again.

'For instance,' she continues, 'in most societies there are laws against cannibalism, and yet when the light aeroplane I and my husband were piloting crashed in the Andes and I was stranded for three months without food, I had to decide whether I was going to observe that law and face certain death, or break the law in order to survive.'

Ms Livingstone pauses. Everybody is listening now. Even me.

'You had to eat your husband?' I say.

She stares wistfully into the distance. Tears form in the corners of her eyes. She brushes them away.

'Perhaps now is not the right time to talk about it,' she says. 'All I'm saying is that sometimes rules have to be broken.'

I check the fingers on her left hand. She's wearing a wedding ring. What a phoney. I bet she didn't really eat her husband. I bet she had a secret stash of muesli bars or something and

she's just pretending that she ate her husband.
She's a fake.

'I thought this morning that I might intro-
duce myself by showing you some slides of my
most recent travels,' she says. 'Can somebody
help me to set up the projector and the screen?'

'I will!' says Danny. He practically leaps
out of his seat and runs to the cupboard to
get the screen out. Definitely not the sort of
behaviour that's going to get him expelled.

While he sets up the screen I lean back on
my chair, turn up my Walkman full blast,
drum on the table with my hands and sing
the guitar solos at the top of my voice.

Ms Livingstone doesn't kick me out
though. She's saying something to the class.
She points at me. They all look across and
laugh. Even Lisa. I don't know what Ms Livingstone said but I don't think they're laughing with me any more. They're laughing at
me. Another one to her.

She turns the lights out and shows a slide
of herself rowing a canoe down a river. On
either side of the river is thick jungle.

I pick up my spitball shooter. The thing I
really like about slide shows is that they give
you a chance to practise precision spitball

EASY HAND
SILHOUETTE
IDEAS.
A DUCK

ANOTHER
DUCK

CHER
(acting as
a duck)

SYDNEY
OPERA
HOUSE

BATTLE
SCENE FROM
BRAVEHEART

Pg 29 and
I feel a
bit flat.

shooting. You only get a little bit of time to hit each target before the next slide appears. I take a deep breath and aim my shooter at Ms Livingstone's pith helmet.

Damn. Too hard. I've blown the shooter right out of my hand. It's landed up near the front of the room.

I get out of my seat and walk down the aisle to retrieve it.

Suddenly there's an enormous crash. I've tripped over the projector cord and knocked the slide projector off the table.

Silence.

Ms Livingstone turns the lights on. She stares at me.

'Please don't feel bad, Andy,' she says. 'It's time for a new projector anyway. That's just the excuse I needed to update. I've always wanted one with a remote-control wheel, but while the other projector still worked I just couldn't justify the expense.'

I pick up my spitball shooter and go back to my desk. Looks like getting sent to the principal's office is going to be harder than I thought. I've still got one last weapon though. Blood capsules!

I take two out of my pocket.

'Danny,' I say, 'pretend to punch me in the mouth.'

'Punch you in the mouth?' says Danny. 'But why? You're my best friend.'

'No, don't really do it,' I say. 'Just pretend.'

'Why?' he says.

SURE-FIRE WAYS TO GET EXPELLED #6

Andy waits with giant scissors to snip the Principal's belt at assembly.

'So that we get into trouble for fighting. I'm going to bite down on some blood capsules and make it look really bad.'

'But I'm not sure I want to get expelled any more,' says Danny.

'What about our deal?' I say.

'But our new teacher is just so cool,' he says. 'She's so interesting.'

'I pity you,' I say. 'She's not interesting. She's a fake. A phoney. She hasn't even eaten her husband.'

'How do you know?' says Danny.

'Because she's wearing a wedding ring for a start,' I say.

Mr Livingstone, who let his wife part-eat him, mimes to the Press.

'Maybe she only ate a bit of him and then they were rescued,' says Danny.

'What—she ate part of him while he was still alive?' I say.

'Yes,' says Danny. 'Maybe they just ate his toes or something he didn't really need.'

'Suit yourself, Dan,' I say. 'Believe what

you want—but if you don't want to get expelled, I'll just tell her that you hit me because I provoked you.'

'Okay,' says Danny. 'If you insist.'

'I insist,' I say.

WHAM!

Danny punches me in the jaw. Hard. I fall to the floor.

'I said to *pretend* to hit me, you moron,' I mumble.

'Sorry,' he says. 'I was trying to make it look real.'

I bite down on the capsules. They've got an awful taste. But I can feel the fake blood flowing out of my mouth and down my neck. I roll around, groaning.

'AAAAGGGHHHH . . .' I say. 'Aaaagggghh-hhh . . .'

Ms Livingstone comes over and looks down at me.

She shakes her head.

'You're not really hurt, are you, Andy?' she says.

'Yes, I am,' I say. 'Danny hit me. But it was all my fault. I asked for it and if anybody should be sent to the principal's office I think it should be me.'

Ms Livingstone leans down and sniffs my breath.

'Blood capsules,' she says, screwing up her face. 'There's no mistaking that smell.'

She is sharp. I'll give her that. 'They're mine,' I say. 'And I don't blame you for being angry. They are against the rules.'

'No, I'm not angry,' she says. 'I'd just hoped never to see another blood capsule as long as I lived. When I worked as a stunt double for Natasha Teasedale I had to chew about fifty a day.'

'You worked as a stunt double for Natasha Teasedale?' I say. 'Which movie?'

'All of them,' says Ms Livingstone.

'Wow,' I say. Oops. I didn't mean to say that. I just meant to think it. 'I mean, sure you were a stunt double . . . sure, sure.'

'It's true,' she says. 'I grew up in a circus and then I got into martial arts. I was spotted by Natasha Teasedale's director at a tae kwon do exhibition in Tokyo, and that's how I got into the movies. Falling out of buildings, fighting wild tigers, jumping out of speeding cars . . . you name it, I've done it.'

That's amazing. I'd love to stay around and hear more about her movie career, and

REX STROMSKI'S NIAGRA IN A BARREL

especially about working with Natasha Teasedale, but I can't. I have to be expelled. I don't want to spend my life sitting around listening to stories about somebody else's adventures—I want to get out there and have my own.

'That's all very interesting, I'm sure,' I say, 'but the classroom is no place for stunt work. You should punish me.'

'Stunt work?' she guffaws. 'You call *that* stunt work? I'll show you stunt work.'

She climbs onto my table. 'Andy,' she says, 'get up here!'

'Me?' I say. 'Up there?'

She nods. She's serious. She means business.

I climb up on the table. That's another rule broken.

'Okay,' she says. 'Now punch me.'

'You mean pretend to punch you?' I say.

'No,' she says. 'I mean really punch me.'

Punch a teacher? That's guaranteed to get me expelled. And not only expelled, either. I'm a pretty hard hitter. I could really hurt her. I could end up in jail. I'd rather stay in school.

'I don't think I should do this, Ms Livingstone,' I say.

'Come on!' she says, pointing to her chin. 'Hit me.'

'Okay,' I shrug, 'you asked for it.'

I swing at her chin. But before my fist can connect with her face she cracks her head back, teeters on the edge of the table for a moment, wobbles, and then, without warning, does a back flip and crashes onto the floor.

The class cheers.

'Now jump down and strangle me!' she says.

'But, Ms Livingstone,' I say.

'Just do it!' she says.

I jump down. I put my hands around her neck. But I don't even get to squeeze it before she lets out a bloodcurdling scream and begins writhing and gasping as if I'm really strangling her. It is very realistic. Not that I've ever strangled anybody, but I'm sure this is what they'd look like if I did.

The door opens and the principal walks in.

I'm gone now.

He looks at the scene—the blackboard graffiti, the broken projector, Ms Livingstone struggling on the floor, and the worst thing of

JUST PRINCIPALS

RARE HAMMERHEAD Principal

Principal with the lot, to go!

SWISS-ARMY principal.

all: me sitting on top of her, my hands around her throat.

'What is the meaning of all this?' he bellows.

I scramble to my feet.

Ms Livingstone stops her act and gets up.

'Oh, hello, Mr Stanley,' she says. 'I was just showing the children some of the tricks of the stunt trade.'

The principal nods.

'Oh,' he says. 'That's all right. I thought something was wrong.'

'No, everything's fine,' she says. 'We've covered falling backwards off a table and now Andy is helping me to demonstrate strangulation.'

'I'm very pleased to hear it,' he says. 'However, I've always felt, and this is just my opinion, that strangulation can be more convincingly simulated if the victim doesn't make any sound. It should all be suggested by the movement of the limbs. Here, let me show you.'

He gets down on the floor, on his back, and starts waving his arms and kicking his legs in the air—like a dying fly.

I can't believe what's happening here. For the first time in my life I am actually learning something interesting and useful at school.

I can't get expelled now. Not until the stunt lesson is over, anyway. And then I want to find out exactly what happened to Ms Livingstone in the Andes. And what it was like growing up in a circus. And I've got a million questions to ask about Natasha Teasedale.

I think I'll get expelled next week instead.

Bogeyboy

I'm cramped.

I'm cold.

I can hardly breathe.

I've been lying underneath my sister's bed for more than an hour now. Where is she? The clock near the front door has just chimed midnight and she told Mum and Dad she would be home by eleven.

It's not exactly a lot of fun down here.

The bed is really low. Every time I take a breath my chest presses against the bottom of the bed. I can't even turn my head without grazing my nose.

So why am I here?

I'll tell you why.

Revenge.

I'm doing it to pay Jen back for laughing at me because I wet my bed. Not that I really did wet my bed—well I did, but it happened because I was trying to put out a fire . . . but it's kind of hard to explain the difference to people like Jen. Especially when they're rolling around on the floor laughing at you.

BOGEYMAN
(TYPE: 1)

BOGEYMAN
(TYPE: 2)

Well two can play that game. Jen might not have wet her bed recently, but she is still scared of the bogeyman. I know this because I overheard her confessing it to her boyfriend. She's convinced the bogeyman lives under her bed and is just waiting for a chance to grab her leg and pull her under. Well, tonight her nightmare is going to come true. When she comes home, I'm going to reach out and grab her ankle. She'll die.

She's out on a date with Craig Bennett. They've been going out together since the school social. I can't imagine what she sees in him. He's got no sense of humour. He tried to punch my head in at the social because I tricked him into thinking I was a girl. How was I to know he'd fall in love with me? Serves him right for being such a sleaze.

THE REALLY OFFENSIVE T-SHIRT SLOGAN can be found on Page 128 The NOT VERY OFFENSIVE T-SHIRT SLOGAN can be found on Pg 118.

For all I know, they probably got home ages ago and have been standing out in the

That was a traumatic experience.

driveway smooching all this time. Maybe I should go and check. I could be wasting an even better opportunity to get revenge on Jen. I could throw a bucket of water over her and Craig. I could ring the police and tell them two suspicious-looking teenagers are hanging around outside. I could get a cardboard tube, stand on the roof of the house and provide a running commentary on the action for the benefit of the neighbours. The possibilities are endless. And a lot more fun than lying here.

THINGS I FOUND UNDER MY BED.

Live old Chewing gum.

Detached Barbie Head (3).

I start wriggling out from underneath the bed. Hang on. What's that?

I hear sounds outside. Footsteps coming up the path. I hear the key in the front door.

Just in time!

I wriggle under again. Not long now.

Smurf (without head).

5 week old decaying sport sock.

Pile of Cotton Buds (with earwax).

In a moment Jen will open her bedroom door. She will click on the light. She will approach the bed. I will reach out and grab her ankle. She will scream. I will roar like a monster. She will scream again. I will roar again—but this time not like a monster. I will be roaring with laughter.

I hear whispering. Jen's room is right next to the front door.

CRUNCH

what was that thing?

'Would you like to come in?' says Jen.

'Are you sure it's all right?' says Craig.

'Yes, of course I'm sure,' says Jen.

'But what about your parents?' says Craig.

'Their bedroom is upstairs,' she says. 'They won't wake up—and even if they do I'll just tell them you're borrowing a CD or something.'

'What about your stupid little brother?' says Craig. 'What if he's still up?'

'Oh don't worry about him,' says Jen. 'He would have been in bed hours ago. He's just a child.'

'Some child,' says Craig. 'I should have taught him a lesson while I had the chance. Nobody makes a fool of Craig Bennett and gets away with it.'

'He didn't make a fool of you, Craig,' says Jen. 'He was the one who looked ridiculous.'

'Yeah,' Craig chuckles. 'Those Action Man undies . . . what a loser.'

They are both laughing. I don't see what's so funny. Action Man's not a loser.

'Come on,' says Jen. 'Just for a minute.'

'Well, okay,' says Craig. 'Just for a minute.'

Damn—still more waiting. I hope Craig doesn't stay for long.

ANDY'S GUIDE TO CRAIG BENNETT

① Pathetic, Gelled Hair.

② Primitive, Gorilla Eyebrows.

③ Dopey, nothing going on in the brain- Eyes.

④ Stupid- who'd want to kiss that- Mouth (liable to dribble in old age).

⑤ Neander- thal Shoulders.

41

Makes me think about life + death

They come into the hallway and close the front door very quietly.

Jen flicks her bedroom light on.

'Come in,' she says. I hear the door click shut.

Oh no. I don't believe it. She's brought him into her bedroom!

If they find out I'm here I'll be in serious trouble. They'll think that I'm spying on them. Craig will want to punch my head in again . . . and this time Jen will probably let him. She'll probably even help him. I've got to get out of here. But I can't. They'll see me.

Jen kicks off her shoes. One comes skidding across the floor and hits me in the left ear. Ouch. I take a deep breath and clench my teeth.

I'm straining my eyes as far around as I can without moving my head to see where they are. I can see their feet. Jen is in the middle of the room. Craig is over near her dressing table.

'Wow,' says Craig. 'Is this a real crystal ball?'

Jen's got this enormous crystal ball. It's practically as big as a bowling ball. In fact if you ask me, that's all it's good for. All it needs is three holes drilled in the top and it would be perfect.

42 And heaven

'Yes,' she says. 'I can see the future in it.'

'Am I there?' asks Craig.

I see Jen's feet move towards the dressing table.

'Of course you are,' laughs Jen. 'I had the best night, Craig. You really know how to make a girl feel special.'

'That's not hard,' says Craig. 'You're a pretty special girl, Jen. Here, this is for you.'

'Oh thank you,' says Jen. 'I love roses. It's beautiful. Just like the ones Dad grows.'

'Actually, it is one of your dad's,' says Craig. 'I picked it on the way in.'

'You shouldn't have gone to all that trouble,' laughs Jen.

'Nothing's too much trouble for you,' says Craig.

I've got to get out of here. Before I throw up. A rose. How corny. What's next? A box of chocolates?

'Ouch!' says Jen. 'It pricked me!'

I see the rose hit the floor. It's not far from my head. If she bends down to pick it up she's going to see me. I wriggle as far away from the edge of the bed as I can.

'Are you okay?' says Craig. 'Here, let me kiss it better.'

THINGS TO DO, TRAPPED UNDER A BED

Compose Poetry

Play imaginary computer games

Dig a tunnel through the wall

Fall asleep

And do snails have souls?

THINGS
NOT TO DO
HIDING
UNDER
A BED.

EAT BAKED
BEANS.

Try digging
a tunnel
through
the floor.

Use your
mobile
phone.

Relive
your great
sporting
moment.

I can see Craig's black leather shoes facing Jen's bare feet in the centre of her Yin and Yang rug. Craig is standing on the white bit. Jen is on the black bit. Their feet are very close. For a few moments there is no sound.

'Oh Craig,' says Jen.

'Oh Jen,' says Craig.

'Oh brother,' I say, only I say it very quietly so that they don't hear me.

Out of the corner of my eye I see movement. There's something coming out of the rose.

Something black.

Something hairy.

Something disgusting.

Something with fangs.

And it's heading straight for me.

This is not good. Not only am I trapped underneath my sister's bed while she smooches with a thug who has threatened to punch my head in on at least two occasions, now I've got a killer spider heading straight for my earhole.

It's not a really big spider or anything, but that makes it even worse. It's the small ones that are really lethal.

What if it gives me one of those bites that

Did you mention soles?

44

Soles? NO!!

never heals? The sort where your flesh just starts dying and spreads over your whole body until you're practically a zombie.

Or even worse, what if it's pregnant and just wants to paralyse me and lay its eggs in my flesh so that when the babies hatch they've got lots of fresh meat to feed on?

My only hope is that Jen and Craig will see it and deal with it before it reaches me. Look down! Look down!

'Oh Craig,' says Jen.

'Oh Jen,' says Craig.

I don't think they're going to look down.

The spider is crawling towards me. It's so close I can see the light glinting off its enormous black fangs. It's coming to get me.

Hang on. Jen and Craig are moving closer to the bed.

Maybe they'll step on it. Come on . . . please . . . please . . .

Craig's feet stop beside the bed.

I can't see the spider any more. I think he stood on it, but I can't tell for sure.

Hang on.

There it is!

The spider is on the toe of Craig's shoe. It's going to crawl up his leg. Excellent!

Great other PLACES TO HIDE in a bedroom.

In the top drawer.

As hat and coat stand.

Under the rug.

In the light fitting.

GRRR!

Well, not excellent for Craig, but excellent for me.

All I have to do now is wait. Sooner or later Craig is going to realise there's a spider on him. He'll freak. Jen will see the spider and go hysterical—she is even more terrified of spiders than she is of the bogeyman. She will scream and run out of the room. Craig will follow, Mum and Dad will wake up, and in all the commotion I will slip quietly back to my room. Simple.

Suddenly they sit down on the bed. The bed gets even lower. It buckles under their weight and pushes against my chest. Great. I'm even more cramped than I was before. I wish that spider would hurry up. I'm going to suffocate down here.

ALIENS WILL NOW READ THE NOT VERY OFFENSIVE T-SHIRT SLOGAN

I feel an itch on the side of my neck, just below my ear, but I can't scratch it because I'm too squashed. I hate that. It's really itchy and the more I can't scratch the more it itches. I can't stop thinking about it. I need to take my mind off it. I'll do my seven times table. One seven is seven. Two sevens are fourteen. Three sevens are . . . um . . . um . . . damn this itch! I can't concentrate. I can't even remember what three times seven is. It's the itchiest itch ever. And it's spreading. Now it's on my cheek.

Hang on. It's not spreading—it's moving. Itches don't move. I don't think it's an itch— I think it's the spider.

Okay. Get a grip. I'm not going to panic. I'm going to stay calm. I can handle this.

I don't know for sure that it's the spider. It could be just a moth. Or an ant. Something harmless.

Whatever it is, I should be able to squash it if I turn my head and press my cheek against my shoulder.

My nose rubs the bottom of the bed as I turn my head.

Not a good idea. Turning my head has made whatever it is move faster.

It's moving up towards my mouth.

I hold my breath. I strain to look down to see what it is. Uh-oh. It's the spider. It looks much bigger close up.

I squeeze my eyes shut and hold my breath. I want to scream, but the spider places a leg across my lips as if to shush me. This is our secret, it seems to be saying, this is just between you and me.

It draws its furry body across my mouth and pauses. My lips are shut tight.

47

Okay. This is not good. But I'm not going to panic. I'll be all right if I don't panic. I have to keep control of myself and not alarm the spider.

Maybe I could blow it off.

I part my lips the tiniest amount possible and start to blow. The spider doesn't budge. It lowers and flattens its body like it's trying to hold on.

I need a bigger breath. I breathe in as deeply through my nose as I can and blow harder. But it's still not enough. For all I know the spider is enjoying this—it must be like standing in front of a warm heater on a cold day.

Suddenly Jen squeals.

'Stop it, Craig!' she giggles. 'That tickles! Stop please, no!'

The bed buckles and thumps down on my chest.

I gasp. Something catches in my throat. I gulp.

Oh no.

I just swallowed the spider!

'Aaaaaggghhhhh!' I scream.

'What's that?' says Craig.

They've heard me, but I don't care. All I care about is the spider.

What if it bites me on the inside? That's worse than getting bitten on the outside. The poison will go straight into my bloodstream. I could be dead within minutes.

I'm gagging and coughing, trying to get it out. I'm too young to die.

'It's the bogeyman!' screams Jen. 'He's under the bed!'

Craig's face appears beside me.

'Bogey*boy* more like,' he says. 'It's your stupid little brother.'

He grabs my arm and drags me out.

But I don't care. He's doing me a favour. I've got to get out of here. I've got to get to a hospital before the poison takes effect. Before the convulsions start.

'Andy!' says Jen.

I try to stand up. It's not easy because I'm so stiff from having been cramped under the bed for so long. Or maybe it's the first sign of the poison setting in. Maybe my whole body will seize up and I won't be able to move!

I stagger to the door.

'Stop him!' says Jen.

Craig strides across the room. He pushes me away from the door and stands with his back against it.

CPR
for annoying
little brothers.
① Make them comfortable.

Lay them flat.

② Clear their airways.

③ Attach pegs to their toes.

④ Insert lots of ice blocks in their pants.

⑤ Paint their fingernails pink.

⑥ I am a Nerd.

In thick black texta write "I am a Nerd" on their forehead.

'Not so fast, buddy,' he says, rolling up his shirt sleeves. 'I think we need to have a little talk.'

Jen gets up from the bed and joins Craig at the door.

'What were you doing under there?' she says.

'Yeah, you little weirdo!' says Craig. 'Explain!'

'I haven't got time to explain,' I say. 'I have to get to the hospital. It's a matter of life or death.'

Craig snorts.

'It's a matter of life or death all right,' he says, 'but you won't need a hospital by the time I've finished with you. You'll be going straight to the morgue!'

'Yeah, you're in big trouble, Andy,' says Jen. 'Wait till I tell Mum and Dad!'

'You do that and I'll tell them you got home late and you had Craig in your room!' I say.

'I'll just deny it,' says Jen.

'But it's true!' I say.

'I know that and you know that,' says Jen. 'But who do you think Mum and Dad are going to believe? Me or you?'

She's got a point but I don't care. I don't

care about anything. I'm going to die.

'Please let me go,' I beg. 'I swear I won't
tell anybody anything. Just let me go.'

Suddenly I feel the most extraordinary
sensation at the back of my throat.

At the back
of Andy's
throat.

'Are you all right, Andy?' says Jen. 'You've
gone green!'

'Probably just another one of his dumb
tricks,' says Craig.

'No,' says Jen. 'Look at him. I think there
really is something wrong.'

I can't speak. I gag and cough. It's like
when you touch the back of your throat to
make yourself sick . . . only it's not me doing
the touching. It's the spider! It's trying to get
out. I gag again. Something flies out of my
mouth and lands on the carpet.

Something wet.

Something furry.

Something disgusting.

We all stare at it. A leg extends from the
furry blob—and another and another and
another.

That is truly gross, but better out than in
I guess.

It starts dragging itself across the carpet
towards the door. Towards Craig and Jen.

Jen screams. Craig screams too. Even louder than Jen.

They both run from the door back to the bed. They are huddled in the corner clutching each other, staring at me in horror.

'Go away!' screams Jen. 'Get out!'

So this is what it's like to be the bogeyman. This is what it's like to have people terrified of you. I could get used to this.

INSIDE ANDY'S HEAD:

① ANDY'S BRAIN

② SPIDER'S EGG SAC.

I make a big show of licking my lips. I look down at the spider.

'Nice flavour,' I say. 'But a bit hairy. Either of you want to try it?'

Jen puts a hand over her mouth. Craig goes white.

'What's the matter?' I say. 'Aren't you feeling well?'

They shake their heads.

I move towards the door. My work here is done.

'Sweet dreams,' I say.

RUNAWAY PRAM

O f all the things I've ever done, this would have to be the most stupid.

I'm lying on my back squashed into a pram. Sucking a dummy. Waving a Porky Pig rattle. Wearing a nappy.

Danny is pushing me down the hill. He can hardly walk for laughing.

'Googoo gaga!' I gurgle.

'Good baby,' says Danny.

We spent the whole morning walking around the streets inspecting the piles of junk left on everybody's nature strips for the hard rubbish collection tomorrow. That's where we found the pram. It's a big old-fashioned one with large wheels, curved mudguards and a high chrome handle. The

ANDY's
genuine
PORKY
PIG
RATTLE.

JUST
DUMMIES

Standard

For
Sharing

for
Twins

For
fussy
babies

Punk
babies

Andy
(what a
dummy)

pram is a bit battered, but it still goes, and it's got great suspension. And as if that wasn't enough, there was a garbage bag full of old baby clothes and toys to go with it.

Putting on a nappy and going for a ride just seemed like the obvious thing to do.

The dummy is starting to taste a bit rubbery. I take a deep breath and spit it out. It hits Danny in the eye.

'Bad baby!' says Danny. He lets the pram go.

I start to roll down the hill. I scream.

Danny grabs the pram.

'Just tricking!' he says.

'Good one,' I say.

He lets go again.

I roll for a couple more seconds, but this time I'm only a little bit worried. He grabs the pram again.

'You're an idiot,' I say.

'What am I?' he says.

'An idiot.'

He lets go again.

I roll faster this time. He lets me roll a few metres.

'Danny?' I say.

He laughs and runs to catch me. But just

54

OH OH
SANDPAPER

as he's about to grab the pram, he trips and falls flat on his face.

The pram takes off down the hill. For real this time.

'Danny!' I yell.

I'm flying down the hill. I'd try and jump out but I'm going too fast. But if I don't jump, I'm going to cross the road at the bottom of the hill and smash into number 21's brick fence.

I see a man watering his nature strip. It's Mr Broadbent, our next-door neighbour.

'Mr B!' I yell. 'Mr B! Help!'

He turns around.

I'm kneeling up in the pram waving my Porky Pig rattle.

'I can't stop!' I yell. 'Stretch your hose across the road!'

He shakes his head and turns back to his watering.

Mr B and I don't get along too well. I know I can be a bit annoying at times, but that's no excuse for ignoring a fellow human being in distress.

'You'll be sorry!' I yell back.

I look over my shoulder at number 21's rapidly approaching brick fence. Actually, I think it's me who's going to be sorry unless . . . unless . . .

I look at the Porky Pig rattle. I can use it as a brake! I reach down and jam it in the wheel spokes. The rattle shatters. Thanks for nothing, Porky.

What do I do now?

I notice that the pram is veering slightly to the right. Maybe if I leaned over a bit more I could get round the corner . . . away from the fence and down the next hill.

That hill is even steeper and it has an intersection at the end. But it does eventually level out, and the traffic shouldn't be too bad at this time of day. It's got to be worth a try.

I lean over the side and look back at Danny. He's running down the hill, but there's no way he's going to reach me in time.

Mr Scribble steps on the moon.

The pram is almost tipping over. I'm on two wheels! Sparks are flying off the wheel rims. But it's working. I hear the sound of metal screaming. I close my eyes. I open them again and look over the top of the pram bonnet. The hill seems steeper than I remembered—but then I haven't seen it from this perspective before.

I hear barking. I look across the road. It's

That was a bit rough.

56

the bull terrier from number 19.

'So long, dog-breath!' I call. He throws himself against the fence.

Everything's going my way now. I've even got a green light at the intersection.

Oh no—I don't believe it!

I *had* a green light.

Now it's yellow.

Now red.

Now I'm in trouble.

The crossroad is full of traffic. On either side, there are cars, buses, trucks and motor-bikes. All ready to take off. Right over the top of me.

I have to make them stop. But how?

I know!

I grab the bag of baby gear and pull out a baby doll. It's pretty wrecked, but it's still very realistic. It might just do the trick.

'Sorry about this,' I say, 'but it's either you or me.'

I throw the doll as far ahead of the pram as I can. It lands right in front of all the traffic.

The cars and trucks squeal to a halt. I rocket into the intersection. There's nothing in my way. Well, nothing except for the doll.

The pram hits the doll and flips up into

the air. I hang onto the sides as it does a complete somersault. Radical! All I have to do now is land safely.

I look over the side of the pram. I'm heading for a fire hydrant.

SMASH!

The fire hydrant casing comes off and a fountain of water sprays out the side. It blasts the back of the pram and sends me hurtling down the stretch of road that I was hoping to slow down on.

I hear a huffing and panting sound behind me. Thank goodness. Danny!

I look around.

Uh-oh.

It's not Danny. It's the bull terrier from number 19. He's broken out and is chasing me. He's gaining on me too.

I grab my bag of baby stuff and pull out the first thing that comes to hand. A plastic bottle. I throw it at the dog. It hits the road and bounces off into the gutter.

I reach into the bag again. I grab something smooth and hard. A container of baby powder. Perfect! I can create a smokescreen that will choke the dog and give me time to disappear.

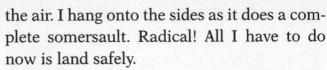

I throw the powder. It hits the ground. The container explodes. An enormous cloud of perfumed white powder billows out behind me.

But it doesn't stop the dog. He runs straight through it as if it was . . . well . . . baby powder I guess. The only difference now is that he's whiter. And madder. And he's gaining on me.

I have to speed up! I've got a strong tail wind. Why not take advantage of it? I remove my nappy. Lucky I left my undies on. There's a wire coathanger in the pram, so I rig the nappy up on a sort of coathanger sail-frame. The wind catches the nappy and I go speeding forwards. Soon the dog is just a speck in the distance.

I hear bells. Uh-oh. Bells can mean only one thing. A railway crossing!

A train is heading for the crossing and the boom gates are coming down. But it's okay. I think I'm going fast enough to make it under the gates and across the tracks in time.

I push the pram bonnet down so it doesn't catch on the gate and duck right down so I don't hit my head.

I come to a sudden stop. I made it under

the boom gate all right, but now the wheels are stuck in the tracks. The train is almost on top of me.

I close my eyes.

This is it. The big one. What a stupid way to go. Sitting in a pram wearing nothing but a pair of undies.

Then, above the dinging of the bell and the roar of the train, I hear the huffing and panting again.

I look up. It's the dog. Barrelling towards me with his head down. He's going to give the pram the headbutt of the century.

'No!' I yell. 'Stop! There's no sense in both of us dying!'

WHAM!

The force of the dog hitting the back of the pram sends me hurtling forwards across the tracks, under the boom gate and speeding off down the road again.

I look behind me. The train is clattering through the crossing. The dog is nowhere to be seen. But I can't worry about him now— I've got problems of my own.

I'm heading towards two men carrying a large sheet of glass. They see me coming. Their faces drop.

60

I veer left so that they can keep going across the road. But they go left.

I veer right to try to squeeze through the gap on the other side. But they go right.

'Get out of the way!' I yell.

Now they're just going back and forth, back and forth, back and forth . . .

I notice a road off to the right. I've got to take it. I lean over to get the pram onto two wheels again.

There is a great crash of breaking glass. I glance behind me. It's the dog! He's just run right through the sheet of glass. He is indestructible. The men are waving their arms and yelling.

'Stop!' they yell. 'Eewayamp!'

What? Are they crazy? Eewayamp? What's an eewayamp?

I turn around. I'm not on a road at all. I'm on a FREEWAY RAMP!

And even worse, I'm heading towards a big red sign that says WRONG WAY GO BACK.

I can't. I'm going too fast. I'm going to be on the freeway in seconds.

But the ramp has a sharp bend. There's no way I can make that turn.

I crash into the kerb. I go flying out of the

Wow! A Prampoline!

pram, over the sign and over the sound protection barrier.

I'm hurtling down into somebody's backyard. This is going to hurt. Think of the biggest and baddest bike accident you ever had and then multiply it by fifteen thousand. Now take that number and raise it to the power of ten. It's probably going to be about seventeen million times worse than that.

I don't believe it! A trampoline.

I land on my stomach and bounce down so hard that for a moment I feel the ground through the thin layer of trampoline rubber. But it's only for a moment. I shoot back up into the air. Away from the trampoline. Away from the backyard and towards a high wooden fence. I think I'm going to make it, but it's going to be close.

I flap my arms to give me extra lift.

I skim over the top of the fence . . . but only just. A nail catches my undies and they're pulled off me as I sail over.

I'm flying through the air.

Naked.

Actually it's not such a bad feeling. In fact it's kind of nice. I can feel the wind on places I've never felt the wind on before.

ANDY's Collection of things stuck on rusty nails.

Piece of Danny's undies.

A piece of Mr Broadbent's brain.

Mrs Grove's nose.

WAAAAAA

And my luck seems to be holding.

I'm heading for a swimming pool!

It seems strangely familiar.

A man and a woman are lying on banana lounges by the side of the pool. They seem familiar too, but I haven't got time to work out why. I have to prepare for splashdown.

I close my eyes and make my body into an upside-down 'V' shape so that I don't go too deep.

SPLASH!

A perfect landing.

I swim to the surface, shake my head and wipe my eyes.

Uh-oh.

Now I know why the man and the woman look familiar.

It's my dad's boss. And his wife.

'Hi, Mr Bainbridge! Hi, Mrs Bainbridge!' I say. 'Just thought I'd drop in.'

I don't know why they are looking so surprised. It's not like this is the first time I've appeared in front of them, without warning, without my pants. There was the time I got stuck in their bathroom window. And the time I fell through the dining room roof. But to be fair, I guess this is the most spectacular.

I really don't like razor blades.

63

'I guess you're wondering how I got here,' I say. 'Well I can explain . . .'

Mr Bainbridge holds up his hand.

'No, please don't, Andy,' he says, getting up out of his chair. 'It's not necessary. I'll just go and ring your father.'

Mrs Bainbridge is holding her hands up to her eyes. Mr Bainbridge helps her up and they go inside.

I kick back and float across the pool.

I can't believe it. I survived. That was the most terrifying ride of my life.

I can't wait to get home, fix up the pram and do it all over again.

me, too

I don't quite feel 100% today.

Food Fight

s far as I'm concerned the only good thing about fancy restaurants is that they have candles on the tables.

'Watch this,' I say to Danny.

I pass my hand slowly through the candle flame and then hold it up to show him the black mark left on my fingers.

'How tough is that?' I say.

'That's nothing,' says Danny. 'Watch this!'

Danny rolls up his sleeve and passes his hand across the flame. But he doesn't keep going. He stops halfway. The candle is burning him. Danny is crazy.

He jerks his hand out of the flame and shakes it back and forth.

'Ouch, ooch, itch, utch, eech,' he says. He

bites his lip and looks up at the ceiling.

'I beg your pardon?' I say.

'Hot,' he says, shaking his hand. 'Really hot!'

Mum gives us a withering look.

'Would you stop that!' she says.

'Stop what?' I say.

'Stop playing with the candles.'

'We're not playing,' I say. 'We're performing amazing feats of bravery and endurance.'

She gives me another withering look. It's even more withering than the last one. In fact it's the witheringest look I've ever received. I'm surprised that the little pink flowers in the middle of the table didn't just keel over and die from it.

'Just don't,' she says.

I sigh and slump in my chair.

I thought tonight would be boring—but not this boring. I didn't want to come, but Mum insisted. She won a meal for four in a radio competition and thought it would be nice to take the family out somewhere special. Jen got out of it because it's her boyfriend's birthday. I said I would only come if I could bring Danny along for company.

I don't think Dad is too thrilled to be here

AMAZING
FEATS
AT THE
DINNER
TABLE

EATING
HOTTER THAN
HOT
MUSTARD

Desperate
attempt
not to
sneeze
with mouth
full of food

THUMP!

Backwards
3½-turn
flip of salt
shaker into
soup pot.

Now, I'm feeling more together.

either. He is fidgeting and drumming his fingers on the table.

'Stop that,' says Mum. 'Do you want everybody to look at us?'

'No,' says Dad. 'Just the waiter. What do we have to do to get some service around here?'

Firstly, attract the waiter's attention.

'Be patient,' says Mum. 'This is a five-star restaurant, not a fast-food outlet.'

'It is for some people,' says Dad, nodding towards a table nearby. 'That couple arrived after us and they've already been served drinks, and they've got menus.'

CHIPS

Always explore the delights of exotic cuisine.

I've got something that will get the waiter's attention. Hanging on the back of my chair is my jacket, and in the pocket is a party popper I brought with me.

WHEN YOUR MEAL ARRIVES:

I reach around to get it, but Danny stops me.

He grabs my arm.

'Hey,' he whispers. 'Isn't that Natasha Teasedale?'

Remember good table manners,

'Where?' I say.

Danny points at the couple Dad was talking about. They are sitting a few tables away from us.

and always spit out the plate.

'No,' I say. 'It can't be.'

67

Would you like to see my snail impressions?

'It is,' says Danny. 'Look at her hair. And that's Dirk Gibson with her.'

The more I look, the more I think Danny might be right. She has curly red hair that cascades down either side of her face and rests in bunches on the table-top. It's Natasha Teasedale all right. Nobody else in the world has hair like that.

'Wow!' I say.

In case you've just crawled out from under a rock, Natasha Teasedale is the biggest star on Australian television. She's been in millions of shows and movies and won thousands of logies. Her boyfriend Dirk Gibson is on television too, but he's not as big a star as Natasha. He's on the wrestling program where big dumb beefcakes pretend to fight each other. Beats me what she sees in him.

'Should we go and say hello?' says Danny.

'No!' I say.

'Why not?' he says. 'Are you chicken?'

'No, I just wouldn't know what to say or do.'

'How about, "Hello"?' says Danny. 'And we could give her some flowers.'

'Where are we going to get flowers from?' I say.

GREAT FEATS AT THE DINNER TABLE #17

NOT THOSE KIND OF FEETS!!

Sucking a glass of lemonade through a Tim Tam.

Sucking an entire thick shake in one breath. (Gasp!).

'From there,' says Danny, pointing to the table next to ours. It's all set up with plates and cutlery and there's a vase of little pink flowers in the middle, but there's nobody sitting at it.

'Okay,' I say. 'Go on.'

'You've got to come too,' says Danny.

'No way,' I say. 'You saw her first.'

'You like her more than me,' says Danny.

'Do not.'

'Do so.'

'But she's with her boyfriend,' I say.

'No she's not,' says Danny. 'Not any more. He just left the table.'

I look over. Danny's right. Natasha is alone. It's now or never.

'Okay,' I say. 'Let's do it.'

We stand up.

'Where are you going?' says Mum.

'We're just going to the toilet,' I say.

Mum looks at Dad.

Dad is cleaning his fingernails with his fork. He puts his fork down, looking guilty. 'What are you looking at me for?'

'Go with them,' says Mum.

'Me?' says Dad. 'Why?'

'Well I can't go,' says Mum.

JUST DON'T!

TOILET
SECURITY
STAFF.

'Actually, we don't need anybody to take us,' I say. 'We're old enough to go by ourselves.'

'Well, don't cause any trouble,' says Mum.

'We're only going to the toilet,' I say.

'No need to use that tone of voice with me,' says Mum. 'You know exactly what I mean. Go straight there. Don't play with the flush buttons. Don't lock the cubicle doors and climb out over the top. Wash your hands when you've finished. Don't have races to see how fast you can empty the soap dispenser. Don't point the hand dryer at your hair and pretend you're rock stars—remember, other people have to use the restrooms as well as you.'

I give Mum a withering look.

'How old do you think I am?'

'Do I have to answer that?'

'Come on, Danny,' I say.

'And don't throw your pants out the window!' calls Mum.

We walk quickly away from the table before Mum can say anything else embarrassing. I don't want Natasha to hear.

'Grab the flowers,' whispers Danny.

I take the flowers from the vase.

Danny and I are both very nervous.

We walk up to Natasha's table. Up close she

70 Egyptian Snail.

is even more beautiful than she is on television.

'Hello,' I say.

Natasha is concentrating on her menu. She doesn't hear me.

I clear my throat and try again.

'Um, excuse me,' I say. 'Natasha?'

She looks up.

'No autographs, boys,' she says with a sigh. 'I'm relaxing, okay?'

'We don't want autographs,' I say. I offer her the flowers, which are dripping. 'We just wanted to give you these.'

Ms Natasha Teasedale looking for a quiet night out.

Her face softens.

'Why, thank you,' she says.

'They're from me too,' says Danny. He reaches across the table to try to give them to her as well. He can be so childish sometimes.

As he reaches, he bumps my arm and I knock over a candle. It falls out of the holder and rolls across the table towards Natasha. The flame connects with her frizzy curls and climbs up her hair in an instant.

This is unbelievable. We just wanted to say hello—not set her hair on fire.

There is an almost-full glass of beer on the table. I pick it up and throw it at her burning hair. It puts the fire out. Apart from being wet,

71

Polite applause.

her hair hardly looks any different. If it wasn't for the smell, you wouldn't even know there'd been a fire. I'm a hero.

'How dare you!' she splutters. 'How dare you throw beer in my face!'

I must have been too quick. Natasha doesn't seem to realise what has happened. Before I can explain, she picks up her glass of red wine and throws it at me.

I duck.

DANGEROUS FOODS:

Sharpened banana.

She looks past me and puts her hand over her mouth. I turn around.

It's Dirk. The wine has gone all over his shirt. He looks like he's splattered with blood.

'Sorry, Dirk,' she says. 'I wasn't aiming for you. It was meant for him.'

Pineapple (radio-active).

'Why?' says Dirk. 'Did he hurt you?'

'He threw beer in my face,' says Natasha.

'He what?' says Dirk. His face goes as red as his shirt.

A lit apple.

He picks up a breadstick. It's a giant one— more like a club than a breadstick.

'I'll teach you to throw beer in a lady's face,' he says.

High altitude napalm strawberry.

'No, you don't understand,' I say. 'Her hair was on fire.'

72 Greek Snail

'You set her hair on fire?' he says.

'Yes,' I say. 'Well, no. I mean I did, but I didn't mean to. I was just giving her some flowers.'

'They were from me as well,' says Danny.

Dirk's face is twisted with rage.

'You tried to give my girlfriend flowers?'

I'm backed up against the table next to Natasha's. Dirk steps towards me. I realise that nothing I can say will calm him down.

I reach behind me for a weapon. My hands close on something soft and oily. I look down. I've got three olives.

'Stop right there!' I say to Dirk.

But he keeps right on coming.

I throw one of the olives at him. He uses the breadstick to bat it clear across the restaurant. It hits the front window and splatters like a bug on a windscreen.

'Andy!' yells Mum. 'Stop that!'

She is standing up, hands on her hips, glaring at me.

'What about him?' I say.

Mum looks at Dirk.

'You stop it too,' she says.

But Dirk doesn't stop. He takes a step towards me.

CHAOS THEORY.

Olive rolls off table

and out the door...

Into the path of a large truck,

tripping the truck. It rolls...

it bounces, it crashes into the moon.
cont. Pg 96.

73 Wild applause.

I chuck another olive. Dirk bats it into the chandelier and sets it spinning. It creates a sort of disco ball effect, throwing little circles of light around the room.

'Stop it, Dirk!' screams Natasha.

'Just let me hit him once,' he says. He raises the breadstick over his shoulder.

I throw my last olive. Dirk bats it straight back at me. It's like a bullet. It hits me in the chest with such force that I am propelled backwards onto a table-top.

I look up. I see the surprised faces of two old ladies above me.

'Excuse me,' I say. 'A little accident . . .'

'Accident nothing,' says one of the ladies. 'It was that brute's fault.'

'I've never liked that Dirk Gibson,' says the other lady, putting a little bowl of pepper into my hand. 'He's nothing but a big bully. Give him this from us.'

'Thanks,' I say. It's just what I need. And just in time.

Dirk picks me up by my collar. He's frothing at the mouth. I throw the pepper into his face. The reaction is instant.

'Ah-ah-ah . . . CHOO!'

Right in my face. I'm blown back across

74

Finnish Snail. Fin land you idiot!

the table. Dirk staggers around blindly and crashes into the waiter who is carrying a tray of drinks.

The waiter stumbles backwards into my dad's lap. Dirk lands on top of them both. Dad's chair collapses and they end up in a sprawling heap on top of him.

'Get off me, you big ape!' yells Dad.

'I beg your pardon, sir,' says the waiter.

'I wasn't talking to you,' says Dad. 'I was talking to that gorilla on top of us.'

'Are you calling me a gorilla?' says Dirk, getting to his feet.

Dad wriggles out from underneath the waiter and stands up. 'On second thoughts, no,' says Dad, brushing himself off. 'Because it's an insult to gorillas. I'd say somebody who picks on people smaller than himself is more accurately described as a coward.'

'Go, Mr G!' calls Danny.

'Shut up, Danny!' says Dad.

'You just made a big mistake, fella,' says Dirk. 'Nobody calls Dirk Gibson a coward and gets away with it.'

'Oh knock it off, Dirk,' says Natasha.

But Dirk's not listening. He is bearing down on Dad. Dad is backing away. He looks

75

behind him at a large display of fruit. He picks up a pineapple.

USING
A
PINEAPPLE
IN COMBAT.

Grasp in
left hand.

'Don't come any closer,' says Dad. 'I've got a pineapple . . . and I'm not afraid to use it.'

Dirk laughs.

'Just try it!' he says.

'If you insist,' says Dad.

Dad whups Dirk over the head with the pineapple. Dirk staggers around looking dazed. His legs buckle underneath him and he slumps to the ground. You can almost see the birds and stars circling above him.

Pull out
pin with
right hand
and insert
pineapple.

'Good one, Mr G!' says Danny.

Mum appears beside us. She has my jacket in her hand.

'Come on,' she says. 'We're leaving. Before you can do any more damage.'

RUN!!

'But what about our food?' says Danny.

'Never mind your food,' says the waiter. He's kneeling on the floor, putting the broken glasses back on the tray. 'I think it's best for everyone if you leave now. There is a fish and chip shop at the end of the street. You might feel more at home there.'

Mum gives him one of her withering looks.

He gives her one back.

Bow
Thai.

76

She huffs, turns and walks straight into an ice bucket on a stand. It clatters to the floor and she falls on top of it. Dad rushes to help her.

Sorry, I'm just stupid.

'Oh no,' says Danny, grabbing my arm. 'Look!'

I turn around.

The noise seems to have woken Dirk out of his stupor. He shakes his head and looks at us.

'Quick,' says Danny. 'Run!'

'Oh no you don't!' roars Dirk.

We are heading for the door. Danny is just ahead of me. We are almost at the cake cabinet near the front register. I look back. Too late.

Dirk leaps and tackles me to the ground. I'm scrambling to get away but he's holding me tightly around my waist, boa constrictor style. He's going to squeeze me to death.

'Help me, Danny!' I gasp.

Danny runs around to the back of the cake cabinet and grabs a pavlova.

'Let go of him!' says Danny, balancing the pavlova on one hand.

'Not until he's learnt his lesson,' says Dirk, squeezing me even tighter.

When your enemy is about to CRUSH YOU TO DEATH, YOU CAN
(a) CALL FOR YOUR MUM!!
(b) Explain to him that you are suffering from the DEADLY EBOLA VIRUS.
(c) CALL For the MICE IN BLACK.

77
Australian Snail.

'Have it your way,' says Danny. 'I just hope you're hungry.'

He pushes the pavlova into Dirk's face. Dirk yells and lets go of me to wipe the cream and strawberries from his eyes. I quickly wriggle away.

Dirk gets up and lunges at Danny.

Danny jumps up onto the cake cabinet, leaps for the chandelier and swings himself clear across the restaurant.

Dirk turns back to me.

I run to the corner, pull a table over and barricade myself in against the wall.

Dirk reaches over the top of the table.

I see a fork on the floor. I pick it up and stab at his hand.

He shrieks and pulls his arm away.

He tries to grab the table and pull it away from the wall. I stab him again.

'For heaven's sake, control your boys,' the waiter yells at Mum and Dad. 'They are destroying the restaurant.'

Dad points at Dirk. 'What about him?' he says. 'He started it!'

'Yeah,' says the lady who passed me the pepper, 'the big ugly brute!'

'He is not ugly,' says Natasha.

I'm the CHIEF FIRE OFFICER from Pg 15 and I object to the violent fork attack shown above... ≥ARGHH≥

78 Not bad, eh?

'You would say that, you floozy!' says the lady. She grabs a bowl of fruit salad and tips it over Natasha's head.

Danny rushes to Natasha's aid.

'Leave her alone!' he says, grabbing the pepper-lady's hair.

'No, Danny!' I yell. 'She's on our side!'

But it's too late. Danny pushes the pepper-lady's face into a bowl of soup. Her friend throws an omelette at Danny. He ducks and it wraps around the head of a man at the next table. The man's wife retaliates by throwing a huge plate of seafood at Danny.

Her throw is wild and the stuff on the tray goes everywhere. Pieces of fish, prawns, crabs, squid, oysters, and lots of other blobby squishy things are flung across the room. Almost everyone in the restaurant is hit by something.

Suddenly everybody seems to be involved. Food is flying in all directions—entrées, main courses, desserts—you name it, people are chucking it. Even Mum is hurling stuff. She's not exactly hitting anyone, but she seems to be enjoying herself all the same.

Dirk smashes a chair against my table. 'Are you a man or a mouse?' he roars. 'Come out and fight!'

American Snail.

Let there
be less
violence.

'Dirk! That's enough!' screams Natasha above the noise.

But nothing will stop Dirk. He is on a mission. A mission to destroy me.

If only I had my party popper.

I look around for my jacket. It's lying on the floor where Mum dropped it when she fell over the ice bucket.

I come out from behind the barricade. Dirk is in such a frenzy that he doesn't see me. I grab a tablecloth and put it over my head.

I crawl towards my jacket.

Somebody is hitting me with something hard.

I peer out from under the tablecloth. It's Danny. He's whacking me with a lobster.

'Knock it off, you moron,' I say. 'It's me.'

'Sorry, mate,' says Danny.

I make it to my jacket and fumble in the pocket for the popper. Got it!

I stand up. Something wet and spongy hits me in the face. I fall down and drop the popper.

I look up.

OK
YOU'RE
DEAD,
GRIFFITHS!!

Oh no, Dirk has seen me. He's seen the popper too.

He dives to the floor. We are both scrabbling

80 Japanese Snail.

for the popper. He grabs it and holds it cen-
timetres away from my face.

'Got you now, you little weasel,' he says.

'Watch out,' says Dad. 'He's got a party
popper!'

'I know that, Dad,' I say, not taking my
eyes off the popper for a second.

'Don't worry,' says Danny. 'I've got you
covered.'

We both look up. Danny is standing on top
of the bar. He's holding a bottle of champagne,
his thumbs poised on the cork. 'Drop it, Dirk!'

Dirk stares at him.

'You keep out of this,' he says. 'This is
none of your business.'

'His business is my business,' says Danny.
He shakes the bottle and takes aim. 'Drop it
or I'll blow you into the middle of next week.'

Dirk hesitates for a moment and then
drops the popper.

'Damn kids,' he says.

He stands up and turns to Natasha.

'Come on,' he says, 'let's get out of here.'

'No way,' she says. 'I'm not going anywhere with you.'

'But . . .'

'It's over, Dirk.'

81

She takes off an enormous engagement ring and throws it at him.

'I was only trying to protect you,' he says.

'That's what you always say,' she says. 'And you always end up making it worse.'

People start applauding. Natasha looks radiant. It's one of the greatest performances of her career—and we're seeing it live.

Dirk bends down and picks up the ring.

'You're all crazy!' he yells, and barges out of the restaurant.

Everybody in the restaurant applauds.

I stand up.

Danny jumps down off the bar and we high five each other.

Natasha comes over to us.

'I just wanted to thank you both,' she says.

'Don't mention it,' I say.

'No, really,' she says. 'I've never seen anybody stand up to Dirk the way you did today. And to think I was going to marry that brute. You've shown me just how violent and bad-tempered he really is. You were very brave and I'd like to give you a reward.'

'No, please,' I say. 'It's not necessary . . .'

'Close your eyes,' says Natasha. 'Both of you.'

I can't believe it! She's going to kiss me!

DO YOU WANT A DINNER DATE WITH NATASHA TEASEDALE? TO WIN TURN QUICKLY TO PAGE 84. →

French snail (cooked)

This is turning out to be the best night of my life. A food fight in a fancy restaurant *and* a kiss from Natasha Teasedale.

Dad steps between Danny and me. 'I helped too,' he says. He closes his eyes and puts his head forward. Mum pulls him back by the arm.

'No you don't,' she says, giving him one of her withering looks.

Natasha giggles. 'What are you waiting for?' she says to me. 'Don't you want your reward?'

DEADLY BREAD STICK

I close my eyes. Life doesn't get any better than this.

WHACK!

I feel a sharp pain on the top of my head.

Extremely dangerous PAVLOVA.

I open my eyes.

She's holding a breadstick in her hand.

'That's for setting my hair on fire,' she says. 'But . . .'

She raises the breadstick and brings it down again.

WHACK!

'And that's for throwing beer in my face!'

Danny is bent over double laughing.

'Something funny?' she says.

'Yes,' says Danny. 'You are. That was brilliant. He had it coming.'

'You want to see it again?' she says, raising

VAROOOM!!!

British racing snail.

KCAHW!!*

* that's
WHACK
spelt
backwards.

SORRY
TOO
SLOW.
HA!
HA!

the breadstick above her head in a two-handed grip.

'Yes please!' says Danny.

WHACK!

She brings the breadstick down again, but this time not on my head—on Danny's. He's not laughing any more. Just standing there with the bottle of champagne in his hand, looking dazed. Natasha drops the breadstick and heads for the door. The waiter runs after her.

'Madamoiselle Teasedale,' he says. 'I am so sorry!'

She stops and turns around.

'It's okay,' she says.

'No, it is not okay,' he says. 'It is not okay at all.'

'No, you're right,' she says. 'It isn't.' She walks back to her breadstick, picks it up and clocks the waiter over the head.

Boy, that's some temper she's got. But it's understandable, what with the pressure of being so famous and having to learn all those lines and act and sign autographs and everything.

She's about to go through the door. Suddenly there is a loud pop. It's Danny's champagne bottle.

84   Domestic Snail.

'Oops,' says Danny.

The cork fires out and hits Natasha fair and square on the side of the head. It ricochets and shoots straight up into the chandelier. The chandelier blows apart and beads of polished glass rain down over the restaurant. It is a beautiful end to a brilliant performance.

Natasha stops, straightens her shoulders, turns around and gives us a look even more withering than one of Mum's withering looks. Then she turns and walks out of the restaurant without saying a word.

Wow.

What a professional.

What dignity.

What poise.

You've got to hand it to her. She's had her hair set on fire, beer thrown in her face, fruit salad tipped all over her, broken up with her boyfriend and just taken a direct hit in the side of the head from a champagne cork, and yet she can still walk out of the restaurant with style.

She's a great actress. There's no doubt about it. And if I ever see her again I'm going to tell her that.

85 HIGH RISE SNAIL

Snail Aid

I'm standing at the entrance to the park, trying to decide whether to go in. I know it's dangerous but I want to get home before the rain starts again and I'll get there a lot quicker if I cut through the park. I hear thunder. I decide to risk it.

I walk through the gate.

I'm not sure if this was such a good idea after all. There are snails all over the gravel path. I have to walk very slowly to avoid stepping on them. If there's one sound I hate, it's the sound of a snail shell being crushed. I reckon I hate the sound even more than the snail does.

But so far so good.

I've almost made it to the pond in the

ARRGHH

Invisible snail.

middle of the park. No crushed snails and, even better, no sign of my enemy. I look up at the old gum tree just to make sure.

But it's there.

The mad magpie.

Waiting.

For me.

I look around to make sure there is nobody else in the park. The place is deserted. That's good.

I open my bag, take out an ice-cream container and put it on my head. I know it's not a good look, but it's better than having a hole pecked in the top of my skull. That's not a particularly good look either.

I take a deep breath and start running.

There is an explosion of swooping, flapping and clicking around my ears.

Even though I've got my container helmet on I'm still scared. What if the magpie goes for my eyes? What if it pecks them out and feeds them to its babies? I'll be able to see myself being eaten.

The magpie seems to be everywhere at once.

There is an especially hard whack on the side of the container.

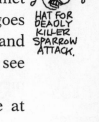

MAGPIE HAT.

HAT FOR ATTACK BY BLACK BIRD.

HAT FOR DEADLY KILLER SPARROW ATTACK.

Stop the impressions.

87

OK!

I stagger sideways.

CRUNCH!

I look down at a grey and brown pasty mess.

A snail! I stood on a snail!

I look up at the magpie. It's getting ready to swoop me again.

'All right,' I yell, 'you asked for it!'

I reach into my bag and pull out my gun.

The magpie is swooping down fast.

I point the gun at it. My hand is shaking. I steady it with my other hand and squeeze the trigger.

POW! POW! POW!

The magpie veers steeply into the air and flies back towards its tree. It's only a cap gun, but the magpie doesn't know that. I blow the end of the gun and slide it into my pocket.

I kneel down and look at the snail. It is blowing bubbles. It's alive.

I've crushed its shell, but not completely. The basic shape is still there. Maybe . . . just maybe . . . I could put it back together again. Like a jigsaw puzzle. It's worth a try.

'I'm really sorry,' I say. 'But don't worry—I think I can rebuild you.'

The snail blows a little green bubble.

DEADLY SPARROW ATTACKING:

They land,

first assault,

the chilling warcry,

they tick,

they explode.

88

That's a good sign. Well, I think it is—sometimes it's hard to tell with snails.

There's a picnic table near the pond. I can use it for the operation. I take my library card out of my pocket. I slide it slowly underneath the snail and lift it up.

The magpie is nowhere to be seen, but I put my hand over the top of the snail to protect it, just in case the magpie tries to launch a surprise attack. I run, crouching at the same time. This is a war zone.

We make it safely to the table. The top of the table is wet and dirty. I fish around in my pocket and find a handkerchief. It's got a huge blob of old chewing gum stuck to it. I was saving it for an emergency—and here it is.

I lay the handkerchief out flat on the table. I bet real surgeons don't have to work under these conditions.

I ease the snail off my library card and onto the handkerchief.

Luckily I've got a glue-stick in my bag. I get it out, but it's hard to know exactly how to start. The glue-stick is jumbo-sized and the pieces of snail shell are so tiny. And the edges are so thin.

I look over at the gum tree to check on the magpie. I can't see it, but I notice that the gum tree has long white pieces of papery bark curling off it. It gives me an idea. I could smear glue onto the bark, wrap it around the snail, and use the strands of chewing gum to hold it all together while the glue dries. Just like a plaster cast.

'Stay there,' I say to the snail. 'I'll be right back.'

I sprint across to the tree.

The bark is wet. I rip a few sheets off to get to the dry stuff underneath.

'Hey you!' says a voice behind me. 'Can't you read the sign?'

I turn around.

A man in green overalls is sitting in what looks like a little golf buggy. He must be the gardener.

'What sign?' I say, backing away from the tree and up onto the grass.

'That sign,' he says pointing at the base of the tree.

I look at the little sign. It says KEEP OFF THE GARDEN.

'Sorry,' I say. 'I just needed some bark.'

'So does the tree,' says the gardener. 'In

fact, the tree needs it a whole lot more than you do.'

'No, you don't understand,' I say. 'It's not for me, it's for a snail . . .'

But the gardener is not interested in my explanation. He's already tearing off across the grass in search of more criminals.

It doesn't matter anyway. I've got the bark. I head back towards the table.

I realise I'm still wearing the container on my head. How embarrassing!

I go to take it off, but suddenly the air is filled with the sound of flapping and clicking. It's the magpie! Back already. I start ducking and weaving, but it doesn't try to attack me.

I look up. The magpie is heading back to its nest. What was that all about?

I reach the table.

I don't believe it.

The snail is gone!

I know what that magpie was up to. It was on a snail-stealing raid. My poor snail is about to become baby magpie food.

But not if I can help it.

I run to the tree and start climbing.

The magpie goes berserk. I bet nobody has ever dared come this close to its nest

91 I'm going to bed.

AHH

before. The bird does a mid-air U-turn and zeros in on me.

I see a small blob falling through the air. My snail!

It splashes into the pond.

This is terrible. The pond is full of gold-fish! My snail is in even more danger than before.

I pull my gun out of my pocket and fire it at the magpie. The magpie flees skywards.

I run to the edge of the pond. There's something going on in the middle. The fish are all in the one spot. They're probably fighting over who's going to eat my snail.

I take off my shoes and roll up my pants. I'm about to wade in when I hear the sound of a motor behind me.

'Hey you!' says the gardener through a megaphone. 'Can't you read the sign?'

'What sign?' I say.

He points to the sign on the side of the pond. It says NO SWIMMING.

'But my snail!' I say. 'I have to save my snail!'

'I don't care if you have to save your mother!' he says. 'The sign says no swimming!'

He tears off again before I can argue. I'm

Good night.

getting really sick of this man and his stupid signs. He just doesn't get it. This is not about saving my mother. This is an emergency. This is about saving my snail. If it's not already too late, that is.

I kneel down and lean forward to look into the pond. The ice-cream container falls off my head and splashes into the water. The fish scatter. I have a brilliant idea. I can use the container to scoop the fish up. I look around to check there's no signs that say NO SCOOPING. No—only one that says NO FISHING. But I'm not going to fish—I'm going to scoop. I grab the container and use it to try to catch the fish, but I can't reach them. The pond's too deep.

Then I have another brilliant idea. I go over to the NO FISHING sign. It is nailed to a wooden stake. I pull the stake out of the ground and remove the sign. I take out the nail and use it to attach my container to the stake. I now have a scoop that can reach right into the middle of the pond. And best of all, I won't be breaking any rules. As far as I can see there is no sign around here saying DO NOT DISMANTLE THE NO FISHING SIGN AND TURN IT INTO A SCOOP.

Andy's fish scoop.

AHH

I scoop my container into the pond and catch two of the biggest and fattest goldfish I can find. One of the fish has big ugly boggle eyes. I pick it up. I peer into the fish's gaping mouth. My snail is stuck in its throat. No wonder the fish's eyes are boggling.

Now I've got the snail—all I have to do is to get it out of the fish. But how? Tickle it? Tell it a joke and make it laugh? What sort of jokes do fish find funny? I'm trying to think of a fish joke when the fish wriggles out of my hand and falls to the ground. It flip-flops around on the grass and the snail pops out of its mouth.

Why did the fish cross the road?

I've heard it.

I throw the fish back into the pond and rush my snail to the operating table.

Amazingly, most of the snail's shell is still there. But there's no time to lose.

I paste little pieces of paperbark over the broken pieces of shell to help hold it all together. I tear some small bits of green plastic off the cover of my school diary and use them to replace the missing pieces of shell.

I stand back and admire my work. Looks cool. A brown and green snail. And not only does it look good, it's great camouflage as well. The other snails are going to be so jealous.

My snail seems pretty happy with its new shell too. It's frothing and bubbling with excitement. Well, frothing and bubbling anyway. Like I said, it's hard to tell with snails.

I wrap long strands of chewing gum around the snail's shell to hold it all together while the glue dries.

Done. Good as new. Better than new. And stronger. I reckon I could whack this snail with a hammer and the hammer would just bounce off. Not that I'm actually going to try it. I've put this snail through enough trauma for one day.

I put the snail down in the grass and kneel beside it.

'Go now, little snail,' I whisper. I want to say more. I want to tell it how sorry I am and that I will never step on another snail for as long as I live. I want to tell it that I will dedicate my life to fighting for the rights of snails so that they can travel the footpaths of the world free from the fear of being stepped on. But I can't say any of this. I'm too choked up.

As I watch it begin its slide to freedom I feel a mixture of awe and pride. I'm like those people who save beached whales. Only I've done more than just save the snail, I've improved it.

CHH

The moon
falls from
the sky,
hitting the
Earth,

which
knocks
Saturn
into the
corner
pocket,
rebounds

sinking
Uranus,

cleaving
the entire
table but
for the
olive.

I'm still waving goodbye to the snail half an hour later when I hear the golf buggy again.

I look up.

Uh-oh. The gardener is over at the pond, looking at my ice-cream container scoop. I left it beside the pond. And the other fish is still in it. Oops!

'What's this fish doing in here?' he says.

'Um . . . would you believe it jumped?' I say. 'I wouldn't be surprised if you didn't believe me because it *was* pretty incredible. I've never seen anything like it before. It just leapt out of the water and landed in the container.'

From the look on his face it is obvious he doesn't believe me.

He picks up my scoop.

'Can't you read the sign?' he barks. He points to where the NO FISHING sign was. He looks. No sign. He looks at the wooden stake in his hand. He looks at the NO FISHING sign lying on the grass.

He turns back to me. His eyes are bulging. He looks a bit like one of the fish. He pours the water and the fish back into the pond and wrenches the container off the wooden stake.

'All right, you troublemaker,' he says. 'I've

HMM

had enough. I want you out of my park!'

'But you don't understand,' I say.

'No *you* don't understand!' he says. 'This
park is my responsibility. All the plants and
animals here are in my care and you are
threatening their wellbeing!'

'But I saved a snail,' I say.

He is not listening. He is walking towards
me slowly, still holding the wooden stake. He
slaps it into the palm of his hand.

'Are you going to leave or do I have to
make you?' he says.

'Now don't do anything you might regret,'
I say, backing away slowly.

'Oh, I won't regret it,' he says, slapping his
hand with the stake again.

I reach for my gun.

'Don't come any closer,' I say, pointing it at
him.

He laughs and keeps right on coming.

I squeeze the trigger. Nothing.

I squeeze it again. Still nothing.

Drat! Out of caps.

I'm about to step back when something
stops me. I look behind me.

My snail.

If I step back I'll squash it. Again. But if I

CHOO

BEST
Worst
Ways
to DIE!

Falling
into a
Mincer.

ARGHH

Being
eaten by
a ladybird.

Bored to
Death by
Hockey on
Cable TV.

Being
run over

by a
Lego bus,
twice.

don't take the step the gardener will get me for sure.

It's me or the snail. I have to take that step. But I can't. I can't do it. I made a promise.

The gardener grabs my collar.

'Gotcha!' he says.

I suppose there are worse ways to die than being strangled by an insane gardener. I'm not sure what they are right at the moment, but I'm sure they exist.

Suddenly there is a flurry of white and black. Clicking and flapping. The magpie! I knew there was a worse way to die.

I can't run because the gardener is holding my collar so tight. I close my eyes and get ready to accept my fate. Any moment that enormous black beak will penetrate my skull and it will all be over. I hope I go to heaven and get a pair of angel wings. First thing I'll do is come back to the park and divebomb the magpie. See how much it likes it.

What's taking so long?

I open my eyes. Just in time to see the magpie score a direct hit. But not on me. On the gardener.

He screams. He lets go of my collar and starts running. The magpie flies up into the

HMMM

air, circles and prepares to swoop him again.

It is a beautiful sight. Almost as beautiful as the sight of my snail still sliding slowly across the grass to freedom. But not quite. Nothing can compare to that.

If you would like to help in the fight for a safer world for snails, please contact Snail Aid at www.andygriffiths.com.au/snailaid.htm

99

CHOOOO

Who Am I?

Voices.

I hear voices.

I open my eyes.

Everything's blurred.

I close my eyes and open them again.

Round shapes against a white sky. But still blurred. And my head hurts.

I feel a hand shaking my shoulder. The two round shapes merge into one and a face appears. It comes in close. I try to make out who it is but the face does not look familiar to me.

'Andy!' says the face. 'Are you okay?'

'Who's Andy?' I say.

'You're Andy,' says the face.

'Who are you?' I say.

The joys of the JACK in the Box.

Uncle Bernie examines the present given to him by his favourite nephew.

'You know me!' says the face. 'I'm Danny. Your best friend. You just got hit in the head. Don't you remember? We were trying to make a jack-in-the-box. You were just about to test it, but it went off in your face. I can't believe you don't remember it.'

Danny? Jack-in-the-box? My head hurts, that's for sure, but I don't remember getting hit. I don't remember anything about a jack-in-the-box. And I don't remember anyone called Danny.

'I don't know what you're talking about,' I say.

'Try sitting up,' he says.

'I think I'm going to be sick,' I say.

'I'd better get you inside,' he says.

He helps me to my feet. The ground is spongy. It's like walking on a mattress.

I look around me. We're in somebody's backyard. There is a clothesline in the centre. It's bent over at a forty-five degree angle, one of the corners practically sticking into the ground. There's a half burned-down fence running alongside the driveway. In the carport there's a mangled pram that looks like it's been run over by a truck. The whole area looks like it should be cordoned off

101

with yellow tape and declared a disaster zone.

'Where am I?' I say.

'In your backyard,' says the boy.

'My backyard?' I say.

He sighs.

'Take it easy up the steps,' he says.

I wobble my way to the top of the porch.

The boy opens a sliding glass door and guides me through it. Inside the house it's dark and cool.

'Mrs G!' he calls. 'Mrs G! Come quick! Andy's been hurt!'

'Who's Mrs G?' I say.

'That's your mother,' he says. 'You must remember your own mother.'

'No,' I say. 'I can't remember anything.'

The boy looks around the room. He grabs my arm and leads me over to a shelf full of photographs.

He points to one of a man and a woman.

'That's your mum,' he says, pointing to the woman.

'And who's the guy with the big ears?' I say.

'That's your dad,' he says. 'But you'd better not let him hear you saying he's got big ears. He goes ballistic.'

JUST MOTHERS: She's the one who:

eats your brussel sprouts for you.

loves to iron your undies.

thinks the sun shines out of you.

my boy.

102

Hmmm. He's obviously got a bad temper. That would explain the state of the backyard.

'Here's a photo of you,' he says.

He's pointing to a picture of a group of people in a restaurant. They are all staring at someone in a gorilla suit. The gorilla has spaghetti all over its head.

I recognise the man and woman from the other photo, but nobody else looks familiar.

'Which one am I?' I say.

'You're the one in the gorilla suit,' he says. 'Remember? You gave Jen a gorillagram for her birthday and she tipped spaghetti all over you.'

'Jen?' I say. 'Who's Jen?'

'Your sister,' he says, pointing to the girl in the middle of the photo.

'She looks nice,' I say.

The boy looks at me closely.

'You really do have amnesia, don't you?' he says.

'I don't know,' I say. 'I can't remember.'

'Mrs G?' he calls again.

Nobody answers.

'The mother must be out,' I say.

'Not *the* mother,' he says. '*Your* mother.

You're really starting to freak me out. Maybe you should go up to your room and have a rest.'

'Yeah,' I say. 'Maybe you're right.'

'Somebody will be home soon,' he says. 'I'll drop by later and see how you are.'

'Okay,' I say. 'But where's the bedroom?'

'Upstairs. The one with the big red skull on the door,' he says. 'You can't miss it.'

'Thanks,' I say. 'I'm glad I met you.'

'Get some rest,' he says. 'I'll see you later.'

I go up the stairs and find the door with the skull on it. Underneath the skull there's a sign that says ANDY'S ROOM. DANGER! ENTER AT OWN RISK!

I walk in.

Wow, what an amazing smell. Sort of like a sports changing room crossed with a rubbish tip. And the mess! It looks like a bomb went off. Not a normal bomb though. One filled with undies, socks and towels. They're everywhere. Hanging off the light, the curtain rails and the desk.

There is a gorilla suit thrown across the bed. A half-eaten banana on the floor. A fish tank full of green slimy water on the windowsill.

And the bookshelves have some very

weird stuff on them. A severed hand. A jar with an eyeball in it. And a horrible pink teddy bear with a human skull for a head.

What sort of boy is this Andy?

I look at a photograph on a pinboard. The boy has his thumbs jammed in the corner of his mouth and his pointer fingers in the corners of his eyes. He is pulling his eyes down and his mouth up. And sticking his tongue out as well. What an idiot.

I look in a mirror. I don't look anything like that. I can't be this boy. Whoever I am, I'm not Andy. Unless . . . I'd better just do a quick check. I rest the photo against the mirror. I put my thumbs in my mouth and my fingers in my eyes and try to pinch my fingers and thumbs together. I stick my tongue out.

The resemblance is uncanny.

But this can't be right! I can't be Andy. He's sick! He's disturbed! Me looking like him is just a coincidence. Yeah, that's it. Just some sort of crazy coincidence. I don't belong here. Somewhere, somebody's probably missing me. I bet they're really worried. I know! I'll ring Missing Persons and see if anybody has reported me missing.

REALLY OFFENSIVE T-SHIRT SLOGAN IS NOW FOUND ON PAGE 39.

If you can't remember your name, just look it up in the phone book.

I go downstairs and find a telephone. I ring up the police.

'Hello,' I say. 'I'd like to see if anybody has reported me missing.'

'I see . . .' says the man on the other end of the phone. 'What is your name?'

'I can't remember,' I say.

'You can't remember?'

'No,' I say. 'That's why I'm ringing you. I think I might be missing and I wanted to see if anybody is looking for me.'

'Is this a prank call?' says the man.

'No,' I say. 'It's not a prank call. I'm serious.'

'So let me get this straight,' he says. 'You're the missing person, are you?'

'Yes,' I say. 'I think so.'

'Can you describe your exact location at this moment?' he says.

'Yes,' I say. 'I'm in a house talking on the telephone.'

'Excellent,' says the man. 'Case solved.'

'Huh?' I say.

'Well,' says the man, 'as far as I can figure it, if you are the missing person in question then you just found yourself, so you're no longer missing. Goodbye.'

He hangs up. That wasn't really as helpful

One day at SCHOOL ASSEMBLY

Introducing the School Principal

Young Women and Men

as I'd hoped. Just my luck to get the new guy. And my head is starting to hurt again.

I sit down on the couch.

There is a pile of books on the coffee table. I pick one up. *Coping With A Problem Child*. I pick up another one. *Your Non-gifted Child*. Under that is one called *Smack Your Child To Success*.

Gee, that Jen must be a real troublemaker.

The glass door slides open. I look up. It's the woman from the photo, the man with the big ears and the girl called Jen. They are carrying plastic bags.

'Well,' says Big Ears, 'don't just sit there— give us some help.'

'Excuse me,' I say, 'who am I?'

'Andy, this is no time for a game of twenty questions,' he says. 'Get up off that couch and help us with these bags.'

'So I'm Andy, am I?' I say.

'Andy,' says Big Ears, 'if you don't get those bags into the kitchen in the next ten seconds I swear I will . . .'

'Okay, okay,' I say.

I was right. He has got a bad temper. Best not to get him too upset. I pick up the bags and put them on the kitchen table.

I'm not going to look in there.

in the

If you have lost your memory:

① Fill your gumboots full of ice and put them on.

② Lie down on top of a big hill,

③ Put a torch in your mouth & wait for dark.

④ Wait till a jumbo jet lands.

'Well, what are you waiting for?' says the mother, sighing. 'The shopping isn't going to put itself away.'

I put my hand into a bag. I pull out a box of washing powder.

'Where does this go?' I say.

'In the cupboard in the laundry,' says the mother. 'Where do you think?'

'Where's the laundry?' I say.

The mother takes the box out of my hands.

'On second thoughts, don't worry about it,' she says. 'It will be quicker to do it myself.'

'Mrs G,' I say, 'you think I'm your son, don't you?'

'Yes,' she says. 'Worse luck!'

Big Ears snorts. 'That's what they told us at the hospital,' he says, 'but I think there must have been a mix-up.'

'Really?' I say. This could explain everything. 'Do you think there's any way of checking?'

'Try the zoo,' says the girl. 'They're probably looking for you right now.'

'The zoo?' I say. I guess it's worth a try.

I turn to the mother.

'Would you be able to take me there?' I say.

'Where?' she says.

108
Something will belt me in the face.

'To the zoo,' I say.

'No!' she says. 'What is the matter with you, Andy? Why all these stupid questions?'

'I've lost my memory!' I say. 'I don't know who I am. I don't know who you are.'

'Very funny,' says the mother.

'It's true!' I say. 'I don't think I'm who you think I am.'

'This is a poor time for another one of your incomprehensible jokes, young man,' says Big Ears. 'You're already skating on thin ice bringing home a report with five E's.'

'Five E's?' I say. 'What's wrong with five E's? Doesn't E stand for excellent?'

The girl snorts.

'Five E's for EEEEEDIOT!' she says.

The mother sighs again.

'What about that talk we had last night?' she says. 'Don't you remember what you promised?'

'No,' I say. 'That's what I'm trying to tell you. I don't remember anything.'

Big Ears screws up his face.

'So let me get this straight,' he says. 'You don't remember anything?'

'No,' I say.

'You don't remember who you are?'

Hickory Dickory Dock The mice ran up the clock,

They pulled off its hands,

Put a spanner in the works,

And set fire to it.

THAT'S JUST STUPID... And it doesn't rhyme!

No it won't.

TERRY D
BY
ANDY G

'No.'

'You don't remember your name?'

'I think it's Andy,' I say, 'but only because that's what everybody keeps calling me.'

'I see,' says Big Ears. 'Well the best cure for amnesia is to do the things you normally do in a familiar environment. That should help jog your memory.'

'But what sort of things do I normally do?' I say. 'I can't remember. What am I like?'

'Well for a start you're really annoying,' says the girl. 'You play really dumb tricks and you do really stupid things.'

'Really?' I say.

The mother laughs.

'No, no, no,' she says. 'That's just Jen having a little joke.'

I was right. That girl is a troublemaker.

The girl looks annoyed.

'But, Mum,' she says. 'It's true.'

'That's enough, Jen,' says Big Ears. 'Andy wants to know what sort of boy he *really* is. And we're going to help him remember.'

'Yes, please,' I say, 'tell me!'

'Well,' says the mother, 'you're very helpful. In fact, you're never happier than when you're helping others.'

110

oh, OK!

'I am?'

'Yes,' says the mother. 'You just love housework.'

'I do?' I say.

'But not just housework,' says Big Ears. 'You love working in the garden as well.'

'Really?' I say.

'And you love being my slave and doing everything I tell you to do,' says the girl.

'I do?' I say.

'YES!' they say.

The mother hands me a pair of dishwashing gloves and a bottle of detergent. 'The sooner you get started,' she says, 'the sooner you'll get your memory back.'

THE ADVENTURES OF .... and ....

(Interactive Comic Strip)

(Hint: see Page 97)

It's 6pm. I've washed the dishes, mopped the floor, cleaned the cars, mowed the lawn, cleared out the gutters, vacuumed every room in the house, cut the girl's toenails and sorted her CD collection into alphabetical order, but nothing has worked. I still don't know who I am. All I know is I'm exhausted.

Big Ears walks across the backyard towards me.

He is holding a biscuit tin and an enormous

111

SMASH!

metal spring with a doll's head jammed on one end. 'I assume this is yours,' he says.

It looks vaguely familiar.

'It might be,' I say. 'What is it?'

'I'm not sure,' says Big Ears. 'Looks like some sort of homemade jack-in-the-box.'

Ah! This must be the one that boy was talking about.

Big Ears forces the spring with the doll's head on it down into the tin and pushes the lid into place.

He tilts the tin towards me.

'Would you like a biscuit?' he says.

I hear someone calling out behind me.

I turn around. It's the boy called Danny.

'Hey, Andy!' he says. 'Feeling better?'

'Not really,' I say.

But the boy's not looking at me or listening to me. He's just staring at the tin.

'Don't open that, Mr G,' he says. 'It's dangerous!'

Too late. It's open. Everything goes into slow motion. The lid of the tin shoots off and whizzes past my ear. The doll's head comes off the spring and hits me right in the middle of my forehead. The spring goes straight up and hits Big Ears in the face.

Everything comes flooding back.

I remember who I am.

I'm Andy. I don't like doing housework or working in the garden. I don't like being Jen's slave. I don't like helping people. I like annoying them. I like playing tricks on them. I am stupid. And I love it.

I hear a moan behind me. I look over.

It's Danny.

He is lying in the driveway. The lid of the biscuit tin is on the ground beside him.

I run across to him.

'Danny,' I say. 'Are you okay?'

He rolls his head from side to side and looks at me with a confused cross-eyed stare.

'Danny,' he says. 'Who's Danny?'

'Dad!' I call. 'Help me! Danny's been hurt.'

But Dad doesn't answer.

I look around.

He is standing in the middle of the yard, his face in his hands.

'Dad!' I call. 'Talk to me!'

He takes his hands away from his face. He looks at me and frowns.

'Dad?' he says. 'Who's Dad?'

Dum-Dum

I'm drawing an invisible line down the middle of the table.

'Cross that line and you're dead meat,' I say.

Danny puts his finger over the line.

'You mean this line?' he says.

I whack my ruler down the line. He's too slow. The tip nicks his finger.

'Ow!' screams Danny.

'I'm sorry,' I say, 'but I did warn you.'

Mr Dobson turns around from the board. He is glaring at me.

'Please stand up, Andy,' he says.

'But . . .'

'*Stand* up,' he says.

I stand up.

Playing with rulers is dangerous. DON'T DO IT

More snails on P. 115 → this → way

'Would you mind telling me what just happened?' says Mr Dobson.

'Nothing, sir,' I say.

'Then what was that noise?' says Mr Dobson. 'And why is Danny bent over double holding his finger?'

'It's his own fault,' I say. 'He crossed the line.'

'What line?' says Mr Dobson.

'The line I drew down the middle of the table.'

'Andy,' sighs Mr Dobson, 'you are acting like a child.'

'I am a child, sir,' I remind him.

'Are you trying to be funny?' says Mr Dobson.

'No, sir,' I say. 'It's a fact.'

Sometimes I wonder about Mr Dobson. Does he think I'd be sitting here if I wasn't a child? I don't see too many adults sitting in on his fractions classes for the fun of it. Not that I would ever point this out to him. I wouldn't want to hurt his feelings. He probably thinks his classes on fractions are the best value entertainment around.

'Facts?' he says. 'You want facts? I'll give you a fact. The fact is that your behaviour is

Young King Arthur tries to pull the ruler from the Rock.

Attila the Hun prepares for battle

Joan of Arc grasps her 1 metre wooden ruler as she leads the French into battle.

ANSWER TO
AMAZING
EYE TRICK
#27 see Pg 42.

As Buddha
once read
on a
Cornflakes
packet:
"To define
is to limit."
So the
answer to
this puzzle
is:
As many
differences
as you think
there ought
to be.

little better than I would expect from a five-year-old,' he says. 'In fact, if you don't start acting your age I've got a good mind to take you down to the Preps' class. How would you like that?'

'But the line was very clearly drawn,' I say. 'And I did warn him.'

Mr Dobson just looks at me. He's frowning. I don't think he understands how important invisible lines are in maintaining order in the classroom. The truth is that Mr Dobson should thank me for helping him keep control of the class because he certainly can't. Mr Dobson is our substitute teacher, but if you ask me, he's no substitute for Ms Livingstone. She's been away for the last two months climbing Mount Everest. I wish she'd hurry up and get back.

Mr Dobson walks up to my table.

'Come on,' he says.

'Where are we going?' I say.

'The Preps' room,' he says. 'I've had enough.'

Nobody dares laugh. It's not the first time he's threatened to send somebody to the Preps' room, but it's the first time he's actually done anything about it.

I collect my books and pencil case.

Mrs Livingstone I presume.

116

'Leave your books,' says Mr Dobson. 'You won't be needing them.'

Of course! Going to Preps might not be such a bad thing after all. It will be easier—and a whole lot more fun—than fractions. I mean, how hard can a bit of cutting, pasting and colouring-in be?

I follow Mr Dobson out the door.

'So long, suckers,' I say over my shoulder to the rest of the class.

I follow Mr Dobson down the corridor and across the yard to the junior school.

'Wait out here,' says Mr Dobson at the entrance to the Preps' building.

He walks down the corridor and knocks on a brightly coloured door.

A friendly-looking woman wearing a long dress with red flowers all over it opens the door. Mr Dobson talks to her in a low voice. The woman nods and smiles.

Mr Dobson motions to me to come closer.

The woman gives me a very sweet smile. She crouches down slightly so we can see eye to eye.

'Hello, Andy,' she says. 'My name is Mrs Baxter. Welcome to Preps. You're just in time for show and tell.'

ANDY's
GUIDE
TO MR
DOBSON

① 3 hairs remain... before deforestation it was brown, now grey (some dandruff).
② lots of hair here, though.
③ 3 o'clock shadow.
④ Dictator moustache (actually long nose hairs).

117

- BOING

This drawing escaped from: The Adventures of Balloon Boy by Jill Groves.

I catch a glimpse over her shoulder of all the kids sitting cross-legged on the floor.

'Cool,' I say.

Mrs Baxter nods at Mr Dobson.

He nods back.

'Behave yourself, Andy,' he says, and walks off up the corridor.

I walk into the room.

All the Preps stare.

Mrs Baxter closes the door behind me and puts her arm around my shoulder.

'This is Andy, everybody,' she says. 'I'd like you all to make him feel welcome.'

'But he's a big kid,' says one boy. 'He's not a Prep.'

The NOT VERY OFFENSIVE T-SHIRT SLOGAN has been stolen by aliens who are holding it captive on Page 46.

'But he's welcome all the same,' says Mrs Baxter. 'Sit down, Andy.'

I poke my tongue out at the kid while Mrs Baxter's not looking.

'He poked his tongue out at me,' says the kid.

'I did not,' I say. 'I was licking my lips.'

Mrs Baxter holds up her hands.

'I'm not interested in your stories, Bradley,' she says.

'But he did,' says Bradley.

'Did not,' I say.

118

'Andy! Please!' says Mrs Baxter.

I sit down on one of the tiny tables.

Mrs Baxter shakes her head.

'No, Andy,' she says, pointing to the floor.

She wants me to sit cross-legged? On the floor?

'But . . .' I say. 'I'm too big to . . .'

'You're part of the group,' says Mrs Baxter. 'Just like everybody else.'

I don't mind spending a day with the Preps, but being made to sit on the floor is going a bit far.

I look for a spot with the boys but there are no free spaces. I have to sit between two girls.

'All right,' says Mrs Baxter. 'Now where were we?'

'It was my turn,' says Bradley.

'Oh that's right,' says Mrs Baxter. 'What would you like to tell us about, Bradley?'

Bradley stands up.

'My grandma,' he says.

'And what would you like to tell us about your grandma, Bradley?'

'I don't like her,' he says. 'She smells funny.'

All the kids laugh.

'You smell funny,' whispers the girl on my right. She pinches her nose.

'Oh yeah?' I say. 'Well you smell funny too.'

The girl starts crying.

'Mrs Baxter,' says the girl next to her. 'Wendy's crying.'

'What's the matter, Wendy?' says Mrs Baxter.

'He said I stink,' she blubbers, pointing at me.

'Is that true, Andy?' says Mrs Baxter.

'No,' I say. 'That's not what I said.'

'What did you say?' says Mrs Baxter.

'I said she smelled funny,' I say. 'But she said it to me first.'

'Two wrongs don't make a right,' says Mrs Baxter. 'You should know that.'

'I know,' I say, 'but . . .'

'I think you owe Wendy an apology,' says Mrs Baxter.

'But . . .'

'Apologise!' says Mrs Baxter, flashing me an ice-cold stare.

'I'm sorry I hurt your feelings, Wendy,' I say.

She sniffles.

'Good boy, Andy,' says Mrs Baxter, all

sweetness and light again. 'That wasn't so hard, was it? Now perhaps you've got something you'd like to share with us for show and tell?'

Talk about being put on the spot. I put my hand into my pocket. All I have is my handkerchief, and judging by its hardness it hasn't been washed in a while. It wouldn't be a pretty sight. I pull my hand out.

'No, Mrs Baxter,' I say. 'I don't have anything. Well, nothing you'd want to see, anyway.'

'Of course we would, Andy,' says Mrs Baxter. 'Don't be shy.'

'I'm not being shy,' I say. 'I just don't have anything to show.'

Mrs Baxter flashes me the icy stare again.

'I think you do,' she says.

'Okay,' I say. 'But don't say I didn't warn you.'

I stand up and pull out my handkerchief. It's moulded into a hard crusty ball. It makes a cracking sound as I unfold it. I hold it up in front of my chest.

The kids screw up their faces and groan. Wendy looks like she is going to cry again.

'Ooooh—yuck,' says Bradley. 'Yuck! Yuck! Yuck!'

121

'Yuck! Yuck! Yuck!' the Preps chant. 'Yuck! Yuck! Yuck!'

'Quiet please, everyone,' commands Mrs Baxter. They stop chanting.

She turns to me.

'Put it away now, Andy,' says Mrs Baxter. 'It's not funny. Nobody wants to see that.'

Well, I did try to warn her. I crush it back up into a ball and sit down.

'All right, show and tell is over,' says Mrs Baxter, obviously keen to move on. 'Everybody please go to their tables.' She looks at me. 'You can sit here today, Andy,' says Mrs Baxter, pointing to a seat next to Bradley.

'Why does he have to sit next to me?' says Bradley.

'Because I know you'll look after him,' she says.

I sit down. I feel ridiculous in this tiny chair at this tiny table. My knees don't even fit underneath it. Bradley runs his finger down the centre.

'Cross this line and you're dead meat,' he whispers.

'Grow up,' I whisper back.

'All right class,' says Mrs Baxter, 'we're going to sing the alphabet. One, two, three.'

The class starts up a monotonous chant.

'A . . . B . . . C . . . D . . . E . . . F . . . G . . .'

I chant along with the rest of the kids. This is more like it. This is the sort of easy work I came for. Bradley's chanting is the loudest.

BRADLEY'S ALPHABET.

A for ANDY

'H . . . I . . . J . . . K . . . ENNEL-MENNEL-BEE . . .' he sings.

'What did you say?' I ask him.

'Ennel-mennel-bee,' he says.

'It's not ennel-mennel-bee,' I say.

'Yes it is,' he says. 'That's the words.'

'It's L M N O P,' I say. 'It just sounds like ennel-mennel-bee when you say it fast.'

'No it's not, you dum-dum,' says Bradley.

'Don't call me a dum-dum, you little shrimp!' I hiss back.

All of a sudden he comes at me. He knocks me out of my seat. I can't believe it. I'm fighting with a Prep. And even worse, he seems to be winning. Somehow he manages to get to a sitting position on top of my chest. He's about to punch me in the nose when Mrs Baxter grabs his hand.

'Stop it, you two!' she says. 'Andy! You should be ashamed of yourself!'

'Me? What about him?' I say. 'He started it.'

B for Bradley

C for Clever

D for Dum-Dum

E for EGG SANGA

I'm just sensible

sniff

SPOT THE DIFFERENCE

① ②

ANS: Pg 127.

Mrs Baxter is restraining Bradley. He is like a little wild animal. Snorting and hissing and kicking.

'Bradley is only young,' she says. 'You're old enough to know better. Get back in your seat.'

The rest of the class is whispering and pointing.

This is so unfair. I feel like crying.

'Maybe you're not ready for whole group work yet,' says Mrs Baxter. 'Why don't you try doing these by yourself?'

She puts a pile of Spot The Difference cards in front of me.

'There are four pictures on each card,' she says. 'Three are the same. One is different. See if you can tell which is the odd one out.'

Mrs BAXTER! Bradley's picking on me... again

ENNEL-MENNEL-BEE

I look at the cards. The top one has four aeroplanes on it. I know one is supposed to be different, but as far as I can see they are all the same.

The rest of the class goes on chanting the alphabet. Every time they come to 'LMNOP' Bradley leans towards me and whispers 'ennel-mennel-bee' really loudly in my ear. He's making it very hard for me to concentrate on my cards.

smells nice.

124

I'm still trying to figure out which plane is the odd one out when the bell rings for recess. I get up to go.

'Hang on, Andy,' says Mrs Baxter. 'Not so fast. Have you finished?'

'Yes,' I say. 'They're all the same.'

'Are you sure about that?' she says.

I look again. The same four planes. All red. All with a little blue circle on the wings.

'Yes,' I say. 'The same.'

'What about that one?' she says, pointing to the plane in the bottom right-hand corner. 'Is it going the same way as the others?'

I can't believe it. It's going a different way!

PLANE ↑
CARDS

ANDY ↓
CARDS

'But how . . . when . . . why . . . ?' I stammer. 'It wasn't like that before . . .'

'Hmmm,' says Mrs Baxter, making a mark in her notebook. 'Looks like another area to work on. Run along now and get some fresh air.'

I go out of the building and am about to cross the yard back to the senior school when Mrs Baxter calls after me.

'Andy! Where do you think you're going?'

'Back to the senior school, Mrs Baxter,' I say.

'No, Andy, that's not allowed,' she says.

VERY OLD
LUNCH BOX
BANANA.

ANDY

'Preps have to stay in the area bound by the building and the big tree.'

'But I'm hungry,' I say. 'I have to get something to eat.'

'Sorry, Andy,' she says. 'But you should have thought about that before you came here.'

I look over at the senior school. All my friends are there. Danny and Lisa are sitting next to each other. Lisa has a bag of chips and Danny is shoving a pie into his mouth.

I can't stand it.

I turn around and go and sit under the big tree with the Preps. They are all eating as well. Biscuits, cheese sticks, muesli bars, donuts—you name it, they've got it. Bradley is eating an enormous piece of chocolate cake. It's almost bigger than his head. And he's got a pretty big head.

'You're not going to eat all of that, are you?' I say.

'Probably not,' he says.

'Can I have some?' I say.

'If you can run fast enough,' he says. He throws it into the middle of the yard.

I run to pick it up. I'm just about to grab what's left of the cake when the dog that

CHOMP!

126

hangs around the schoolyard comes out of nowhere and wolfs it down. I feel like I'm going to cry again.

The bell rings and we all go back inside.

In the classroom there are counting blocks laid out on a table. There are two different types of blocks—elephant blocks and chicken blocks.

'Now it's time for maths,' says Mrs Baxter. 'I have two elephant blocks and three chicken blocks. If I take one elephant away, what do I have left?'

Oh that's so easy! I put up my hand but Bradley beats me to it.

'One elephant and three chickens,' he says.

'Very good,' says Mrs Baxter. 'And if I take one chicken away, how many do I have left?'

Easy again! I shoot my hand up.

'Andy?' says Mrs Baxter.

'One elephant and no chickens,' I say.

'Don't you mean one elephant and two chickens?' she says.

'No,' I say. 'You might think you would have two chickens left, but it's a bit trickier than that. See, even if you took only one chicken away you'd still end up with no

127

ANSWER TO SPOT THE DIFFERENCE:
① Andy.
② Block of Wood.
There is No difference. (Although the block of wood is useful....)
Things that can be made from block of wood:

Door knob

Pineapple

Porky Pig rattle.
But with an Andy you can make:

A bottle opener.

Dunny brush.

Doorstop.

chickens because the elephants would stomp on them.'

'I don't think you quite understand, Andy,' says Mrs Baxter, making another note in her book. 'We're not talking about real elephants and real chickens. These are just counting blocks.'

Everybody laughs. I hate Preps.

After a bit more counting it's time for art.

We have to draw a picture of our house and family. Now this is something I *can* do.

I look across at Bradley's picture. It's really bad. Wonky walls. Stupid colours. The sky is green, the people are all the wrong size and shape, and he's even got a purple dog flying around in the sky. I could do a better drawing than that with my eyes shut, but I'm not going to take any chances. I'm going to do something really impressive.

I use my ruler to draw the sides of my house so that they are dead straight. I rule a perfectly pointed roof with a chimney sticking out the side. I draw a little curly wisp of grey smoke coming out of the chimney and colour the sky blue, the grass green and the sun yellow. It's the best drawing I've ever done. Good enough to hang in an art gallery, I reckon.

128

'Mrs Baxter,' calls Bradley. 'Andy's copying me.'

'I am not,' I say.

'Are too,' he says.

'That will do,' says Mrs Baxter. 'Copying somebody else's work is very naughty, Andy.'

'I wasn't copying,' I say.

'He was,' says Bradley.

Mrs Baxter picks up the two drawings and studies them. They look nothing like each other. Anyone can see that.

'See?' I say. 'I didn't copy his.'

'No,' says Mrs Baxter. 'You're right. You didn't copy. Your picture is very different to Bradley's.'

'Yeah,' I say. 'He's got stupid purple dogs flying around a green sky. And his walls are wonky! Look how straight mine are! And everything is the right colour. Mine is much better than Bradley's.'

'Both of your pictures are very good,' says Mrs Baxter. 'Bradley's picture may not be strictly realistic, Andy, but it's very creative. You could learn a lot from Bradley. Try to work more from your heart and less from your head.'

I feel like crying again. But this time I

don't just feel like crying. I actually burst into tears.

Mrs Baxter puts her arm around me.

'You haven't got off to a very good start today, have you?' she says. 'Maybe you'll do better tomorrow.'

ANDY AFTER ONE DAY OF PREPS.

'I won't be here tomorrow,' I say. 'I'm just here for the day.'

Mrs Baxter looks concerned.

'The day?' she says. 'Mr Dobson didn't say anything about this being just for the day. He said I was to keep you here until you were ready to go back up. And, quite frankly, Andy, I just don't think you are ready yet. In fact, I'm not sure how you got up there in the first place.'

I'm sorry Andy, but Preps is for life.

'But . . . but . . . but . . .' I blubber.

'Now come on, Andy,' she says. 'Cheer up. If you apply yourself and work really hard, you'll be back up with the big children before you know it. And, meanwhile, I'm sure Bradley will enjoy looking after you and being your special friend. Won't you, Bradley?'

Bradley nods.

I'M JUST STUPID.

'Yes, Mrs Baxter,' he says. 'I'll look after him.'

I look around at all the colourful posters

130 GASP!

on the walls and the cheery decorations. There's a big pink octopus in the corner and two teddies in a hot-air balloon hanging from the roof. And at the side of the room there's even a little hook with my name on it. I guess there are plenty of worse places I could be.

I sit down. I wait until Mrs Baxter's back is turned and I draw a line down the centre of the table.

I grab Bradley by the collar.

'Cross that line and you're dead meat,' I say.

He nods.

There are going to be a few changes around here.

Chubby Bubbies

It's Lisa Mackney's birthday party. Lisa and all the girls are in the corner of the room looking at her presents. Danny and I are standing at the food table staring at the biggest bowl of marshmallows we have ever seen.

'Bet I can fit more marshmallows in my mouth than you can,' says Danny.

'Bet you can't,' I say.

'Wanna make a million dollar bet?'

'No,' I say.

'Why not?' says Danny, looking disappointed.

'You haven't got a million dollars.'

'I don't need a million dollars,' he says. 'Because I'm going to win.'

'As if!' I say.

'Am too,' says Danny.

'Are not,' I say.

'So are you in?' says Danny.

'No way,' I say.

'Suit yourself,' says Danny. 'You're out!'

'But I wasn't in!'

'All right,' says Danny, 'if you're going to whinge about it then you're in—but I'm warning you, you're testing my patience.'

He picks up a marshmallow from the bowl.

'Danny!' I say. 'For the last time, I'm not playing Chubby Bubbies.'

Danny's face drops.

'You're just trying to act mature in front of Lisa,' he says.

'Am not,' I say. But he's right. I've been trying very hard to be mature and grown-up since I ended up in my undies in front of her at the school social. It's been going pretty well too. Not that she's talked to me that much, but she did invite me to her party, which is a good sign.

'Know what else I think?' says Danny.

'What?' I say.

'You're a wuss.'

How to act Mature (for Cheapskates).

Gel your hair. If you don't have gel, mashed banana will do.

Shades: Use a texta to colour in your dad's old reading glasses.

Just don't smile. It's cheap and you look mysterious.

SNAIL BAIT!

'Am not,' I say.

'Wussy boy, wussy boy,' chants Danny. 'Andy's a wussy boy.'

'Quit it,' I say.

But Danny doesn't let up. He's getting louder and louder. There's only one way to stop him.

I take a marshmallow from the bowl and put it in my mouth.

'One Chubby Bubby,' I say.

Danny looks me in the eye and smiles. He takes two marshmallows from the bowl and puts them both in his mouth.

'Two Chubby Bubbies,' he says.

It's on.

I take two marshmallows from the bowl and put them in my mouth. The marshmallows are making my mouth water, but there's no way I'm going to swallow them. I can't afford for Danny to start singing the wussy boy song again. Lisa might hear him.

'Three Chubby Bubbies,' I say.

'Four Chubby Bubbies,' says Danny.

I look across at Lisa and the other girls. They are busy with the book I gave Lisa for her birthday. It's called *How To Find Your Perfect Partner Through Palm Reading*.

It's not a very good book because when I checked my palm against the picture of the perfect lover's palm it looked nothing like it. It does now, though. I fixed the picture up with a black pen. When Lisa comes to check my palm—which I know she will because girls are very curious about that sort of stuff—she's going to discover that I'm her perfect partner!

But first I have to shut Danny up.

'Come on,' he says. 'Your turn!'

I put two marshmallows in my mouth.

'Five Chubby Bubbies.'

It's getting very hard to say 'Chubby Bubbies', but then that *is* the point of the game.

Danny picks up a handful of marshmallows. He counts them out and stuffs them all into his mouth.

'Ten Chubby Bubbies!' he says, although it sounds more like 'dem dubby ubbees'.

I take an even bigger handful. I poke them one by one into the corners of my mouth. Way down into the bottom of my cheeks. One by one into the space between my gums and the top of my lips. I flatten them and paste them across the roof of my mouth. One underneath my tongue. Others moulded around my teeth.

135

'Fifteen Chubby Bubbies!' I say. Only it doesn't sound like that. It doesn't sound like anything . . . well, nothing human anyway.

I've got to admit that I'm feeling pretty proud of myself.

Greg Box likes to stuff his ear full of ibis.

Danny's eyes are wide. He's wondering how he's ever going to top my effort.

Somebody taps me on the shoulder and I almost swallow the lot. That was close.

I turn around.

It's Lisa and Roseanne. Lisa is clutching her book.

'Hi, Andy,' says Lisa, 'are you having a good time?'

Benny Mussolini likes to see how many pencils he can fit into the holes in his head.

Why does she have to pick now to start talking to me? Right now, when I've got fifteen marshmallows in my mouth? I can't talk to her because I would have to swallow them—and I can't swallow them because I'll lose the competition and owe Danny one million dollars. But I can't not talk to her because, well, she's the most beautiful girl I've ever met. And I can't let her find out that I've stuffed my mouth full of marshmallows because then the most beautiful girl I've ever met will think I'm more of an idiot than she already does.

EEEEEE

I do the only thing possible.

I nod.

Pretty rude to just nod when somebody asks you if you're having a good time, I know, but maybe she'll think I'm just the strong silent type.

She smiles.

'That's good,' she says. 'Have you had something to eat?'

Palm Reading

If only she knew the truth.

I nod again.

Lisa frowns.

'Are you all right?' she says.

I nod for a third time. I give her the thumbs up and try to smile appreciatively without letting the fifteen marshmallows erupt from my mouth.

'Can I ask you something?' she says.

An idea comes to me.

I can't swallow the marshmallows, but maybe I can take them out for a while. We can resume the game later.

Enya O'Brian swallows butterflies.

I pretend that I'm going to sneeze.

'Ah . . . ah . . .'

I turn away from the table.

'Choo!'

I 'sneeze' the marshmallows into my right

137

hand, wipe my mouth and turn back to face Lisa and Roseanne.

'Bless you,' says Lisa.

'Thanks,' I say. 'What did you want to ask me?'

She blushes and looks shy.

'Can we see your palm?' she asks.

'Sure,' I say.

I hold out my left hand.

She shakes her head.

'No, I need your right hand,' she says.

Mrs Peters eats cockroaches.

I can feel the wet stickiness of the fifteen half-chewed marshmallows dripping through my fingers. It's not a nice feeling. I don't think Lisa really needs to see this.

'You don't want to see my right hand,' I say.

'Yes I do,' she says. 'The book says that the right hand gives a more accurate reading.'

'Not in my case,' I say. 'My left hand is much better. Isn't it, Danny?'

He nods. It's not like he can really do anything else.

'Andy,' says Roseanne, 'just show us your right hand.'

I'm going to have to show them my hand.

But not with the marshmallows.

Please IGNORE this SIGN!

I turn away from them, slip the gooey mess into my jacket pocket and wipe my palm on my jeans. I hold it out flat.

'Thank you, Andy,' says Lisa.

She takes hold of my hand. It is still moist and sticky from the marshmallows, but she doesn't seem to notice. She's too busy comparing it with the picture in her book.

Wayne Grotzki tries out his new handset.

'Good heartline,' says Lisa to Roseanne.

'Strong lifeline,' says Roseanne to Lisa.

'This is very promising,' says Lisa. She gives me the most beautiful smile and lets go of my hand. She's obviously noticed the similarity between my palm and the picture in the book. Funny about that.

Lisa and Roseanne rush back to the other girls.

THINGS YOU CAN'T SAY WITH A MOUTHFUL OF MARSHMALLOWS:

psychiatrist
puffer fish
sausages
choo choo
TRY IT!!

Danny shakes me. He points at his mouth. He points at my pocket. He points at my mouth. He wants to get on with the game.

'Okay, okay,' I say.

I take the molten mass out of my pocket. It's not quite as white as it was before—there's blue fluff and bits of sand embedded in it. But unappealing as it is, I have to put it back in my mouth—the thought of owing Danny a million dollars is much worse.

139

mphh mvooph ooppff *

A rough * translation: "gnff loopfff grffff".

I cup my hand over my mouth and suck the marshmallows back in. It makes me want to be sick, but I stifle the urge.

Danny is holding up six marshmallows. If he can put all of them in his mouth he will be one ahead of me. He pushes them in with ease. The interruption has given him an advantage. His marshmallows have melted more than mine. But that's fair. It was me who stopped.

'Thithsteen thubba ummees,' he says, white juice spilling out of the corners of his mouth.

I take another two marshmallows and squash them in my palm to make them as small as possible. I poke them into my bulging mouth.

'Thebentee ubby ubbas,' I say.

Seventeen! This must be a world record. Danny will never beat this.

But he pushes another one into his mouth. And another. And another. And another. That's twenty! That's incredible. But I'm not through yet.

I push one in. My bottom jaw feels like it's going to come apart from my top jaw.

I push another one in. My head is going to explode. My eyeballs are going to pop out.

HA HA. fooled you!!

I push the twentieth marshmallow in. It pops straight back out. I pick it up and use the straw from my drink to push it as far into my mouth as I can.

I've done it! We're even! I'm about to try for twenty-one when I feel another tap on my shoulder.

'Andy?'

I turn around.

It's Lisa again. With her book.

'Sorry,' she says. 'I just need to check your mount of Venus.'

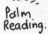
Palm Reading.

She grabs my hand and pokes the fleshy part at the base of my thumb.

She looks back across to the girls.

'It's true!' she calls. 'It's true!'

The girls all come running over.

Lisa displays my hand to them.

'See?' she says, holding up the picture in the book as well. 'The same!'

'Let's have a look at his other hand!' says Roseanne.

She grabs my left hand.

'A perfect match!' she announces.

Lisa beams.

I can't believe how well she's fallen for my trick. I only wish I didn't have twenty

141
That was trick snail bait.

marshmallows in my mouth. I think I'd be as happy as she is.

'You have to kiss now,' says Roseanne. 'Come on, Andy, kiss Lisa!'

Somebody throws a handful of glitter over us.

'Lovers!' they cry.

Lisa closes her eyes and puts her cheek forward. It is the most beautiful cheek I have ever seen. It is like the cheek of a princess in a fairytale. It is a lovely pink colour and the glitter is making it sparkle.

I want to kiss her.

I really do.

But I can't.

What I really want to do is sneeze. For real this time. I think a bit of glitter has gone up my nose. And when you're holding twenty marshmallows in your mouth and you're standing in front of the most beautiful girl in the universe, that's a bit of a worry.

I've got to swallow.

I've got to swallow before I sneeze.

But I can't. It's like trying to swallow a wet face-washer. I've simply got too much in my mouth.

I try to turn away and put my hands over

WARNING!! Book's nearly over.

my mouth like when I did the fake sneeze, but I can't. Lisa's holding my right hand. Roseanne is holding my left.

'Ah . . . ah . . .'

There's no stopping it. I wrench my left hand away from Roseanne and try to put it across my mouth in time.

'Choo!'

Too late.

The marshmallow mush comes leaping through my fingers. It's like the white foam on the edge of a breaking wave.

'He's frothing at the mouth!' screams Roseanne. 'He's got rabies!'

The remains of twenty half-chewed marshmallows have gone all over the front of my shirt, my jeans, my shoes and the carpet.

At least they didn't go over Lisa.

Correction.

At least most of them didn't go over Lisa. She hasn't noticed yet but a glob of marsh-mallow goo has landed right in the middle of her cheek. It looks a lot like—well I won't say—but it comes out of the back end of birds.

Everybody is staring at me.

'You poor thing,' says Lisa, rubbing my back. 'Are you feeling okay?'

Hey! She thinks I'm sick! Maybe this is not so bad after all.

I bend over double, and groan.

'Must have been an off marshmallow,' I say.

I look up.

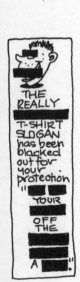

Danny is dancing around the room.

'I win!' he cries. 'I win!'

Everyone is staring at him.

I'm trying to signal to him to shut up—to let him know that I'll concede victory if only he'll shut up. But he doesn't take the hint.

'What do you mean, Danny?' says Lisa, puzzled.

'You spew, you lose,' says Danny. 'And he spewed!'

'I did not spew,' I say. 'I sneezed.'

'Same difference,' he says. 'You owe me a million bucks!'

'What are you talking about?' says Lisa. 'What did you win?'

'Chubby Bubbies!' says Danny. 'Twenty marshmallows each. But he couldn't hold his!'

As what has happened dawns on everybody, their looks of sympathy turn to disgust.

Danny starts up his victory dance again.

STICKFIGURE ANDY
INTERACTIVE
MOVIE:
JUST GRAB
+FLICK

HEY! The book's nearly finished. I can rest.

'Twenty marshmallows,' he sings. 'Twenty marshmallows.'

I fold my arms, roll my eyes and shake my head.

'He is so immature,' I say to Lisa.

'He's not the only one,' says Lisa.

What can I say? How can I make her understand that I didn't *want* to play Chubby Bubbies? That Danny left me no choice?

'I know what you're thinking . . .' I say.

'You do?' says Lisa, picking up a marsh-mallow and squeezing it between her thumb and fingers. 'What am I thinking?'

'You're thinking that I'm really immature and gross and disgusting . . .'

'That's right,' says Lisa. 'But that's not all.'

'It's not?'

'No,' she says. 'I also think you've got a very big mouth.'

'Right,' I say.

'But not as big as mine,' she says.

Lisa puts the marshmallow into her mouth without taking her eyes from mine.

'One Chubby Bubby,' she says.

145

WHAT PEOPLE SAID ABOUT *JUST TRICKING!*

'Mad, fun and way out there!'
DISNEY ADVENTURES

'Entertaining tales of pranks and mischief will have the kids giggling with delight'
THE AGE

'*Just Tricking!* with its anarchic, irreverent style has few literary pretensions. It is a book to read for fun'
MAGPIES

WHAT PEOPLE SAID ABOUT *JUST ANNOYING!*

'Over the top tales from a born story-teller'
MAGPIES

'The stories are far-fetched and imaginative—every young trickster will love them'
AUSTRALIAN BOOKSELLER AND PUBLISHER

'Original, funny and lots of fun'
SUNDAY MAIL (Brisbane)

'This boy needs some discipline!'
SUN-HERALD (Sydney)

'Children aren't going to learn much of any benefit from this book—in fact, they may pick up a few tricks you wish they'd never learnt'
CAIRNS POST